An Augathella Spring

ANNIE SEATON

Augathella Short and Sweet: 3

Copyright © 2023 Annie Seaton

All rights reserved.

ISBN 9781923048133

AUGATHELLA SHORT AND SWEETS

An Augathella Surprise

An Augathella Baby

An Augathella Spring

An Augathella Christmas

An Augathella Wedding

An Augathella Winter

An Augathella Ball

Following on from:

THE AUGATHELLA GIRLS

Book 1: Outback Roads –The Nanny

Book 2: Outback Sky – The Pilot

Book 3: Outback Escape – The Sister

Book 4: Outback Winds – The Jillaroo

Book 5: Outback Dawn – The Visitor

Book 6: Outback Moonlight – The Rogue

Book 7: Outback Dust – The Drifter

Book 8: Outback Hope – The Farmer

CHAPTER 1

Emily

Emily Jansen parked her small station wagon outside the grocery store at the top of the main street in Augathella. She glanced across to the back seat and was rewarded with a beautiful smile from Ophelia, wide-eyed and happy in the baby seat.

Emily opened her door, climbed out, and went around to the passenger side to open the back door. 'You're awake, my sweet,' she said. 'You're such a good girl, not a peep out of you for the last two hundred kilometres. You've had a huge sleep. I'll bet you're hungry, darling.'

There was plenty of food in the camp fridge in the back of their station wagon, and she was thankful that Troy, her late husband, had set the fridge up in the car a couple of years ago. It had made her trip down from Townsville so much easier, being able to have fresh food for both her and Ophelia, and not having to stop frequently to buy food. However, she was getting quite low on supplies and did need to top up here, but first things first.

Emily unclipped the seat buckles and lifted out her little girl. Her skin was warm as Ophelia nestled into her neck. 'Mum-mum,' she said.

'Yes, darling, Mum-mum is here, and we just have to go and see a lady, and then we'll go over to that park and have some lunch.'

Emily had smiled when she'd seen the name of the park across the road—Meat Ant Park! She was certainly not in the tropics now and that suited her just fine.

The grocery store was surprisingly busy even though there were no other cars parked outside. Once inside, Emily soon realised that elderly people who lived in town must walk from their homes with carry bags.

Feeling guilty about going in just to ask a question, Emily went to the fridge near the counter and took out two litres of milk. There would be room for that in the camp fridge.

She walked across to the counter and stood behind the two elderly women waiting. An animated conversation was taking place.

'The new girl is doing an amazing job,' the shorter one said.

'No, Beryl, that's not the new girl I meant.'

'Yes, it is. That young one who bought old Reg's place out on the highway. Apparently, the café is going great guns and they say it's always busy.'

Emily had noticed the Vintage Tea Shop on the highway on her way in; there had been several caravans and quite a few cars parked there. If there was one thing she missed, it was her daily brewed coffee. It was a bit hard to do that with a camp fridge while staying in cabins and caravan parks. Stopping for a coffee had tempted her, but she knew she had things to do first.

'Yes, and do you know what she's decided to do?'

'No, Gladys, but I'm sure you do.'

The patient voice held irritation. 'Beryl, someone has to keep an eye on what's happening in town. You know, I couldn't believe it when old Reg went into the home. I never thought he would. He's been sitting outside that pub for a lot of years, you know.'

'Yes, that's all very well, but tell me what this news is you're busting to tell me.'

'Well, you know Jenny Riley's Spring Garden party that she has every year with the CWA?'

'Yes, I've already started baking for it.'

'Well, Beryl, this year that newcomer out at the tea shop has almost taken over. She's decided to put a big sign out the front saying "CWA fundraiser for the RFDS. Come into town and get your coffee and cake."

Beryl nodded. 'That's good of her.'

'Yes, that may be, but don't you think she's a bit new in town to be getting involved in our town things? She's not a local yet. But the big thing, Beryl, is that Jenny Riley isn't calling it a spring garden party anymore.'

'She has to call it a garden party.'

'Absolutely. That's what it is, and that's what it's always been. Well, apparently, this Jenna girl reckons that if she makes it a little bit more modern, she's going to get all those caravans that have been coming into her tea shop.'

'So, what's it going be called?'

'It's going to be called the Spring Fair.'

Beryl shrugged. 'I suppose I can live with that.'

'I'll be saying my piece at the committee

meeting, trust me! And for the life of me, I don't know why we have to have the meeting out at that girl's new tearoom! What's our town coming to! She'll be running for mayor before we know it.'

Emily hid a smile when she saw the other lady roll her eyes.

'That will be fifty-six dollars, Mrs. Tingle,' the cashier said. Gladys handed over her cash, and as the girl packed up her two bags of groceries, Gladys shook her head. 'Whoever thought I'd be paying twenty-five dollars for one bag of groceries. I don't know what the world is coming to. Do you, Beryl? With all this COVID stuff, somehow people are putting up all the prices of our groceries.'

Emily switched off as the conversation continued, and Beryl was served by the cashier. Finally, it was her turn, and she stepped forward and put the two litres of milk on the counter. The two older ladies, Gladys and Beryl, were still standing near the door, having a conversation about the state of the world. The cashier smiled at Emily and gestured her head towards them.

'Don't worry too much about them, dear. Gladys always has something to whinge about. Just the milk today, is it?'

'Yes, please.'

'Just passing through?' the woman asked.

'Well, I did want to ask you something. I noticed there's no real estate agent in town. In fact, I thought there'd be a little bit more of a shopping centre here.'

'Love, we've got very little here these days. Sign of the times. You could go up to the rural store behind Anderson's garage if you're looking to buy a house. They've got a few for the Charleville agents in their window.' Her eyes narrowed as she regarded Emily.

'No. I'm just perhaps looking for a local

rental.'

'Good luck with that. Town's full at the moment; a lot of investors have bought up the real estate and are renting it out to the stockmen on the properties and the road workers working out on the highway upgrade. I sort of know what's available most of the time, but I really can't think of anything at the moment.'

Emily's heart sank. Her contract at the local primary school started after the spring holidays, and she really needed to be settled before then, plus she had to find somewhere for Ophelia to go during the day. As much as she hated the thought of leaving her with a stranger, Emily needed the work. When she'd seen the one-term part-time contract position at the local primary school advertised in the state education gazette, she'd somehow known this little town in southwestern Queensland was exactly what she needed.

Troy's money—*their* money—hadn't come

through yet. Probate was taking a long time, and her solicitor said that while the manner of his death was being investigated, matters were even more complicated and the process slower.

Emily's throat closed, and she swallowed, refusing to dwell on those issues. Augathella was a new start, and she was going to do the best she could to move on. She *would* find somewhere to live in this town. The contract was only for ten weeks, and then she'd decide where she was going to go next.

'I heard the ladies talking about the tea shop out on the highway,' she asked quietly. 'Do they do coffee out there as well?'

'Do they do coffee? I'll say! Jenna makes the best coffee anywhere I've been in, love. Even though I'm working in this little town, I've had coffee in most places around Australia when Gary and I travelled around in our caravan. Jenna does a great job, and her cakes are amazing.'

'I might give it a try,' she said.

'You won't be sorry.'

Emily handed over the cash for the milk and walked outside.

The woman called Beryl stepped forward 'Hello, love. I couldn't help overhearing your conversation with Dawn in there. I know there's a room available in one of the three units down in Nelson Street. But you'll have to share.'

Gladys raised her eyebrows. 'Who with, Beryl?'

'Well, it's that young Alana who came to town with Jenna. She's moving on.'

'Oh, is she? That girl did most of the baking at the tea shop, I heard. Made the best cakes. If she's left it's doomed unless someone else can keep up to her standard. Where is she going?'

'Don't you worry about that now. And you're wrong. She didn't cook. Young Jenna does her own baking.'

Beryl turned back to Emily. 'I heard you say you were thinking about going out there for a coffee. You ask for Jenna. I know she's got a spare room in her apartment, love.'

Emily nodded. As much as she hated half the town already knowing that she was looking for somewhere to live, it *would* make it easier if she had some inside information. 'Thank you very much, ladies. I'll do that.'

'What a beautiful little girl.' Gladys reached over and tickled Ophelia under her chin and was rewarded with a little chuckle. 'She's a sweet-looking little one, love.'

'Yes, she is, isn't she? Thank you, ladies. I appreciate your help.' Emily put her head down and walked to the car. Maybe moving to such a small town hadn't been such a good idea.

CHAPTER 2

Jenna

'I'm really, really sorry to leave you in the lurch, Jenna. I know I said I'd stay for a while when we moved here, but—'

Jenna put a hand up. 'Alana, It's fine. Rory's been given this great opportunity, and I don't mind at all. I've got more help here than I need, and the business has settled down now that the local interest has eased off a bit.'

'But it's still going alright, isn't it?' Alana asked.

'Between what I'm getting from the caravanners going past on their travels and the locals who are stopping in as they leave Augathella to go down to Charleville to work every morning, it's really good. Besides, I don't mind easing back a bit. We've worked hard setting up plus it gives me time to think about Jenny Riley's Spring Fair. Will you come back for that?'

'How long away is it?' Alana asked.

'Two weeks, but you don't have to. It's such a long way to travel from Moree back up to here.'

'No, it's not.'

Jenna chuckled. 'You're turning into a real bushie, Alana. Where's the woman who found it too hard to drive from Burleigh Heads to Surfers Paradise to work?'

'Yes, I know, but it's different out here. The roads are great to drive on, there's no traffic, and I really enjoy driving with Rory.'

'I think you just enjoy being with Rory.'

'I do, and listen, what's happening with you and Luke?'

Jenna shrugged. 'There is no me and Luke. I think we're just going to be friends. I like him a lot, but he hasn't been here for a couple of weeks.'

'But is there a spark?' Alana looked hopeful.

'No, I don't think so. I've never had a spark so I really can't tell. Anyway, I know he's been busy up in the Northern Territory.'

'You'll know straight away when you meet someone and there's a spark, trust me.'

Jenna chuckled. 'We're just friends.'

'But you do fancy him, don't you, Jen?'

'Um, not in that way.' Jenna shrugged. 'He's a nice guy, but look, I'm busy with the business. I don't need to complicate my life with a partner. And like I said, no spark.' She folded her arms.

Alana regarded Jenna, a frown on her face. 'Seriously, just don't let the business take over your life like you did at the real estate office back on the coast. Look what happened there. Make some time for being happy and socialising.'

'I'm my own boss here. I'm the only one with expectations. I have never been as happy as I've been since we got here. The community is lovely, I've made lots of friends, and I'm loving my little business. I will miss you though, Alana. When do you leave?'

'In the morning. Is that okay with you?'

'Of course it is. You've stocked up the freezer to last me for ages, thank you. Sophie's happy to come in for a couple of days a week, and Ellie, one of the high school girls who worked for us at the opening is leaving school at the end of term this week. I've looked into getting a school-based traineeship for her. She wants to be a pastry chef. I know I haven't got the qualifications to supervise her, but she can do her work hours here and go to TAFE in Charleville.'

'Sounds like it's all working out pretty well.'

'Yes, Ellie is a lovely young girl, and she enjoys working here.'

Alana shook her head. 'It surprises me that

the young ones in town stay local after they leave high school. I know we've seen the coast and we've had our years of going out on the town, but you'd think that after growing up here in this quiet little town, they'd want to spread their wings a bit.'

'Different strokes for different folks,' Jenna said. 'She's happy. Just wants to get her qualifications; she might move to the city then, who knows? Anyway, it's all getting organised. It's not definite yet.'

The tearoom was calm and quiet that morning, and that gave Jenna a good chance to get herself organised. She did a stocktake of the freezer, cool room and pantry and planned to close the doors around two-thirty when the lunch rush stopped. They were having a quick committee meeting for the Spring Fair and then she'd go into town after that to stock up on supplies and maybe do some baking at home tonight after she'd visited Reg.

'Here's another customer. Do you want me to look after them?' Alana said, looking out at the car park. She was rolling pastry for a last batch of the mushroom tarts that had been so popular with the tourists.

'No, it's fine, I'll go out. You keep cutting out those pastry circles. I hate doing them.' Jenna took off her apron and washed her hands.

A pretty woman with long blonde hair stood by the counter, holding a small toddler in her arms.

'Do I need to be seated or can I sit anywhere?' she asked quietly.

'No, you can choose a seat wherever you want, and then I'll come across and take your order. Would you like me to get a high chair?'

The woman smiled. 'Do you have one?'

'I sure do,' Jenna chuckled. 'Not that many of the grey nomads have babies with them, but we do get some Sunday tourists who come up from Charleville with little children.'

The woman nodded and smiled. 'That explains your little colouring corner over there; I wondered about it.'

'Take a seat, and I'll be back in a moment with the chair.' Jenna went to the storeroom beside the cool room that Rory and Kirk had set up for her and lifted out the small wooden highchair. She took it into the kitchen, gave the plastic tray a quick wipe down, and then carried it into the front tearoom. The woman had taken a seat by the window where she could see the garden. Jenna was proud of the beautiful blooms that had started to appear over the last couple of weeks. She and Jenny Riley had worked really hard on that garden, and it was looking beautiful. It amazed Jenna what grew out here: a riot of snapdragons, candytuft, and delphiniums edged the borders in front of the roses that were in heavy bud.

The only thing she was worried about with the lack of rain was that she didn't want to use too much of the tank water to keep the garden going. If it came to it, she'd order water in a truck because the garden made her tearooms that little bit extra special and caught the attention and comments of many grey nomads on their way past. Some of the women over the last couple of weeks had said that they'd stopped specifically to have a coffee because of the flowers. So, even if she had to pay for the water to keep the garden lovely, it would be worthwhile. Jenna made a mental note to follow that up this afternoon.

She carried the high chair across to the table, and the woman stood, lifting the little girl in.

'Hello, sweetie. What's your name?' Jenna asked.

'This is Ophelia,' the woman said.

'And how old is she?'

'She's eighteen months.'

Jenna sensed that the conversation was closed off, and the woman didn't particularly want to talk. Sometimes, some of the customers who called in wanted to talk for ages about the tearoom, the types of tea, and coffee, and the gifts. Who made them, and who helped her in the garden. Other times—and Jenna was very good at picking up when someone just wanted to place their order—there was no need for conversation. This pretty young mother was one of those. Jenna took her order with a smile and headed to the kitchen. She knew when to leave customers in peace.

****

When she took the coffee out, Jenna introduced herself, and her new customer smiled briefly.

'I'm Emily.'

Business became brisk. Jenna lost count of

the caravans, pulling up one after the other for the next hour and a half. To her surprise, Emily stayed at the table the whole time. She refilled her coffee twice and had no problem when Emily asked if she minded if she brought Ophelia's food from the car and fed her at the table.

'Not at all, we're pretty easy-going here,' she said.

'It's just so good to have a highchair again,' Emily said with a little smile.

Jenna left Alana on the coffee machine and took the orders as it got even busier. She was aware of Emily watching her, and it was almost as though she was sizing her up.

Eventually, the rush receded. The vans pulled away, and it was time to start thinking about cleaning up and closing for the afternoon, but Emily still sat there. She was nursing the little girl, who had gone to sleep on her shoulder.

'Would you like another cup of coffee?'

Jenna asked.

'No, I'm fine, thank you. Look, I hope you don't mind me sitting here.' Emily looked up and met Jenna's eyes.

Jenna looked back, unable to ignore the depth of sadness in Emily's eyes.

'I had an ulterior motive for coming here,' Emily said. 'I went into town looking for real estate agents to see if there was somewhere I could stay in town.'

'There's a pub there with rooms, and they're quite nice,' Jenna said.

'No, I need somewhere to stay for the whole school term,' Emily said. 'I'm on contract at the local primary school for ten weeks until the Christmas holidays, and I need somewhere to stay. When I was in town at the IGA, at the grocery store, I met two ladies called Gladys and Beryl.'

Jenna smiled. 'And you managed to escape?

It's a wonder you're still not in there with them, with them probing your entire life history.'

Emily's face closed, and Jenna realised she'd said something wrong. 'Anyway, what did they tell you?' she hurried on.

'They said that, and I'm assuming it's you, that the owner of the tearooms had a room that might be available to rent.'

Jenna looked at Emily, sizing her up. 'I do.'

'And is it available?' Emily continued. 'It's just the two of us, just Ophelia and me. Ophelia is the most well-behaved little darling.' Emily's eyes filled with tears, and a pang of sympathy hit Jenna squarely in the chest. She knew that Emily was sad, and the way she spoke and looked at her daughter reinforced that sadness, and she'd said she was alone.

'So, you're working at the primary school. A few of my friends are teachers there. I think you'll be happy there. It's a very nice little school, very social.'

'Yes, but my immediate problem is finding somewhere to live,' Emily gestured her head down towards the sleeping baby. 'And I need to find some daycare for Ophelia.' Her eyes welled with tears again. 'As much as I hate it, she will have to go to daycare while I work.'

Jenna's heart went out to her. 'Well, then you don't have to worry about somewhere to stay because I certainly have a room. I can give you references and my solicitor's details if you want to speak to somebody to check I'm okay.' She smiled.

'No, it's fine.'

'I'm gone all day, so you'd have privacy and I'm often gone at night. I usually eat at the pub. The last thing I ever feel like doing when I get home from working here all day is cooking a meal in the kitchen, so I barely use the kitchen at home, although I am going home tonight to bake.

28

My assistant, the one who made your great coffee, was sharing the house with me when we moved here from the Gold Coast. But Alana is leaving town with her new partner. So, Emily, you're welcome to stay with me until you get yourself settled. If that suits us both, that is.'

Jenna added that bit because she didn't want to leave herself open to someone moving in who wasn't going to work out.

'Oh, thank you, Jenna. You have no idea how relieved I am.'

'Would you like to come and have a look this afternoon? If it suits, you can move in today, if you like. Or are you staying somewhere else for the time being? Have you just driven up from Charleville for the day?'

'No, I drove south from Longreach today,' she said.

'You must be exhausted. No wonder the poor little one has gone to sleep.' Jenna couldn't help reaching out and touching the soft curls on the little girl's head. 'She's beautiful.'

'She is, she's my beautiful girl,' Emily said.

CHAPTER 3

Jenna

Jenna crouched in the garden at the bottom of the steps, and as she pulled on a particularly tough weed, the sound of an aircraft engine filled the air. She'd put the closed sign up and she was waiting for the committee members to arrive. Never one to waste a minute, she'd decided to weed the garden at the bottom of the stairs while she waited. Jumping up, she brushed her hands on her jeans and then looked up. Disappointment filled her as she realised it was a small plane flying over and not Luke's helicopter.

Jenny Riley had arrived early for their committee meeting and was working at the far end of the garden bed. She stood at the same time Jenna did.

'Time for a cuppa, love?' she asked, and then

her gaze lifted to the sky. 'That'll be Amelia's brother.'

'Amelia's brother? I didn't know he was coming today.'

'Yes, he's got his own plane. She said he does some mustering up in the Northern Territory. We must make sure that he catches up with Fallon when he's here. Apparently, they knew each other in Darwin.'

Jemma nodded and pulled her gardening gloves off.

'You've been quiet this week. You okay, love?'

'Yeah, I'm good. Just a bit tired. Everything's settling well. The new girls are working out, and I finally managed to coax Sophie into not turning up here so much. It doesn't do her good being on her feet all the time.'

'She loves it though.'

'So do I.' She glanced up again. 'I've been half expecting Luke to arrive this week. He hasn't been for a couple of weeks.'

'Have you heard from him?' Jenny asked.

'Not since the week before last.' Jenna shrugged. 'Mum told me to call him before they left yesterday.'

'Oh, that's why you're quiet; your Mum and Dad finally went.'

'Yeah, but they're only going up to Longreach and Winton to have a look around and then they're coming back for a couple more weeks. Mum said she wouldn't miss your garden party for the world.'

'Yes, the Spring Fair is getting close. We've got a lot to do in the next two weeks. We'll get everything allocated at the meeting today.' She turned as three cars came into the car park. 'Here they are now.'

Jenna put her hands on her hips. 'I don't

know what you're doing helping me weed my little garden when you should be working on yours.'

'It looks after itself,' Jenny said happily. 'I went out this morning and gave it a little light spray. The buds are beautiful. They don't need too much water; I don't want them falling off. It's just about perfect.'

'You make sure to tell me how I can come and help on the day or closer to the day. I can close up here.'

'You'll do no such thing,' Jenny said. 'You can't get a reputation for not sticking to business hours. People might drive here specially and find you closed.'

Jenna scrunched her face up. 'Yeah, I guess you're right, but I'll get the girls to work when you need me and I'll make sure everything is right. I'll spend the day and the evening before helping you get ready. And I'm going to bake for you too.'

'I think you've got enough baking of your own to do here, haven't you?'

'Yes, but it's not hard to make a double batch.'

Jenny smiled. 'It would be nice to have some of your sponge cakes. I've never met anyone that makes them just like you.'

'That's my pleasure. Come on, let's go and wait upstairs for this lot.'

'I'll put the kettle on.'

Jenna hurried up the steps and listened as the rumble of the plane faded. She wasn't sure what was going on with Luke. Mum had told her last night not to stress about it.

But Jenna was worried that maybe Luke was keener than she was.

She bit her lip as she went into the kitchen, got the large kettle and put it on the gas stove. She leaned against the countertop, waiting for the kettle to boil as she heard Jenny greet the committee girls and take them to the back tearoom.

Luke was an enigma. She liked him enough but was worried that he'd read too much into their relationship. He was always good to be with, and when they were together, he was totally considerate, but their relationship had never gone beyond a chaste kiss goodnight. Maybe she was reading more into it, maybe Luke just wanted to be friends too. When she'd said that to Mum last night, Mum shook her head, 'A friend who flies his helicopter hundreds of kilometres to come and visit you? He's certainly not coming for a cup of tea.'

'He has to come up here anyway for work, Mum, so he's just being kind. We're just friends.'

'But do you really *like* him, Jenna?'

'I do, he's a really good guy, but there's no

36

point starting a romance because he lives so far away. Who knows, when he finishes with these properties, he might not have to come back here anymore.'

'Yes, and you're settled here, I think. I see what you mean. You certainly don't want to uproot all that if you did have a relationship and had to follow him to where he lives.'

'No chance of that.' Jenna had laughed. 'You're jumping the gun, Mum. We are *just* friends.'

She and Luke had exchanged mobile numbers, and after the first couple of weeks of coming up to visit her, Luke had started to ring her three times a week. They had lots of lovely long chats on the phone at night, and she began to look forward to seeing him again. After a while, she asked him when he was next coming up, and he said he couldn't commit to a date. Jenna realised that maybe that was the brush-off, but the strange thing was he kept ringing, so she didn't know what was going on. She wasn't in a hurry to figure it out, though. She had enough to keep herself occupied with the tearooms, and now that Mum had gone away for a week, she was keeping an eye on Reg too.

The kettle whistled, and she reached for the container of tea leaves. She filled the teapot that she knew Jenny liked. Maybe when Luke called next time, she'd ask him outright what was going on, and then she could stop worrying. Meanwhile, there was a Spring Fair to organise.

***

'Okay, ladies, I now declare the meeting officially open.' Jenny Riley sat at the head of the table in the smaller tearoom at Jenna's Vintage Tearooms.

Jenny had booked the room especially for the meeting because it meant Jenna could be there.

'Thanks for letting us have the room, Jenna.'

'My pleasure. I didn't want to miss out.' Jenna looked around the table and smiled. Sophie and Amelia, both very pregnant, sat together at the end of the table. Opposite them were Beryl and Gladys, and beside them were Fallon Ingram and Callie Cartwright. Laura, Dr Harry's partner, sat at the far end.

Jenny had formed a new committee for her revamped Spring Fair and was keen to get some fresh ideas for the day.

'Thanks for coming, and thanks for your input so far,' she said. 'I'd just like to recap what everyone has said to me already because it's happened in bits and pieces, meeting some of you in the street, having phone conversations, and exchanging text messages. So, to confirm, we're right to go two weeks from this Saturday. The CWA is putting us under their organisation, so we'll be insured for the event, and as usual, all profit will go to the RFDS.'

There were nods and murmurs of assent around the table. Jenna relaxed; she'd been a little worried about Gladys Tingle. She'd heard that she could be a bit of a gossip and troublemaker. She paid attention as Jenny continued.

'This year, we're having a bit of a change. We've decided not to have any jumping castles or pony rides for the kids. Instead, we are thinking about getting a clown and having face painting.'

Callie raised her hand. 'I hope that's not because of what happened to Petie last year, is it, Jenny? I'd hate to think that we are depriving the kids of those fun things because of that. That was purely and simply an accident and was caused by the wind, not by any neglect or anything like that.'

'I know,' Jenny said, 'but that accident

rattled us all. So, I took a look at our work, health, and safety guidelines. It's a Spring Fair, for selling plants, having cups of tea, and getting to meet up with some locals. We'll just have that one little thing for the kids.'

'What about the pony rides?' Laura asked. 'They were really popular last year.'

'Oh, Craig Wilson said that he's happy to bring his ponies in. But again, I guess I'm just a little bit nervous.'

Sophie spoke up. 'How about we put it to a vote, Jenny? It seems pretty harsh to drop all these things that have been a part of the garden party since I was a kid. And I know a lot of the primary school kids are looking forward to it, aren't they, Callie?'

'Yes, they've already started doing some drawings in class, and I know our three boys are really keen. If we make it less attractive to kids, there'll be a lot of disappointed families around.'

Jenny bit her lip and looked around the room. 'Well, I guess we should put it to discussion, and then we'll take a vote.'

Gladys sat up straight and pursed her lips. 'I'm afraid I agree with Jenny. It's a garden party. I don't even like the term "Spring Fair" because that makes it sound like a sideshow alley. This is a fundraiser for the RFDS, and I think we should just sell plants. In fact, I don't even think we should have afternoon tea or have raffles and the 100 Club.'

Jenny shook her head. 'No, Gladys, there will be afternoon tea. There always has been. I've already got the tables and chairs organised, and we've had lots of volunteers to make cakes.' She looked over at Jenna. 'Jenna is even closing the tearooms for the day, so we'll get more passing trade from the highway. She's kindly agreed to put up a banner directing people into town. Has it been delivered yet, Jenna?'

'The banner's ordered, and I'm expecting it to be delivered later in the week,' Jenna replied.

'You'll be right to put it up along your front fence on the highway?' Jenny asked.

'I will, Jenny. Amelia's Ben said he'll come and help put it up as soon as it's delivered.'

'He's just waiting for your call, Jenna,' Amelia said.

Callie leaned forward. 'Okay, I would like to move that we accept Craig's offer of the pony rides, have face painting, and include the clown. I think that will cater to most of the age groups. I don't think we need to have the jumping castle, though.'

There were lots of nods around the table. Gladys sat up straight and pursed her lips. 'It's a garden party, not a children's show,' she insisted.

Jenna said, 'But it's all about raising money for the RFDS, and if we don't have things for the kids, we're not going to get the parents to spend money.'

'You don't know this town as well as we do.' Gladys glared at Jenna.

'And yes, we know that the children like to be involved. It's also a good lesson for them,' Sophie said quietly.

Amelia added, 'I agree.'

The vote went ahead, and all but Gladys smiled when it was agreed to include the children's activities.

Once the meeting was over, Jenna stood to go back to the kitchen, but Amelia called her. 'Jenna? A favour?'

Jenna waited as the other women headed out to their cars. 'Sure, what's up?'

'I'll wait outside for you, Amelia,' Laura said. 'I've got plenty of time. Harry's in Charleville for the day.'

'Thanks, Laura. I'll only be a minute.'

'Are you okay, Amelia?' Jenna thought Amelia had looked a bit pale during the meeting. In contrast to her pale face, Sophie's cheeks were pink, but Amelia had looked a bit drawn.

'I'm fine. Bump's good.' She patted her tummy. 'I had a checkup yesterday and everything's on track. I'm just a bit stressed. We're picking my brother up at the aerodrome tomorrow, and I was hoping you could save a table for us for lunch. I think we'll come but I can ring you if we have to cancel.'

'Jenny thought that was him arriving before.'

'No, he's coming tomorrow.'

'Sure, not a problem. But why would you be stressed? Don't you get on?'

'We used to, but things are pretty rocky in my family. Too detailed to go into now while Laura's waiting, but one day I'll tell you all about how I came to Augathella.'

'I'll look forward to it.' Jenna put her hand on Amelia's arm. 'And the table's not a problem, I'll keep it free for the day in case you want to stay longer.'

'Thank you. And if I pull faces at you when we're having lunch, come and rescue me!'

'I can do that.' Jenna chuckled.

As Amelia hurried out to the car park, Jenna shook her head. Of all the people to have family issues, bright and bubbly Amelia was the last person she would have expected to have a difficult family. She was such a sweet person. Her grandfather had a soft spot for Amelia, and Reg'd been chuffed that she'd been to visit him at the aged care facility a couple of times since he'd moved in.

If her friend needed rescuing tomorrow, Jenna would step right in. She had already taken a dislike to Amelia's brother and she hadn't even met him.

CHAPTER 4

Emily

Emily took more notice of the little town when she drove in after leaving the tearoom. Jenna had given her the address of her apartment block and told her to do a drive-by to see if it suited her. Emily didn't say that a tarpaulin under a tent would suit her at this stage. She was desperate; she needed to find somewhere to live quickly, and that would be the first problem solved. Then, she had to find somebody to look after Ophelia once she started at the school.

The town was a little bit busier than when she had driven in earlier. Two buses came around the corner as she stopped at the stop sign. Children waited in a line outside the primary school. As she did a recce along that street, they appeared well-behaved and were all in uniform.

That was a plus. For a moment, she considered stopping at the school and going into the office to talk to the principal, but she realised it would be too hard with Ophelia. She'd have to wait until she had someone to look after her. It would be very unprofessional to turn up without an appointment, dragging along a little toddler. She and Mr Hamblion, the principal, had had a long conversation on the phone when he'd called to offer her the one-term contract.

She turned left at the end of the school street and went down two blocks of older-style houses. The grass in front of each was dry and brown, but the occasional green shoot was trying to push up towards the late spring sunshine. Most of the yards had small gardens, and an elderly lady on a walker waved and smiled at Emily as she drove slowly past. Calm descended on her like a blanket. She had chosen well, and if only she could get a sitter for Ophelia, everything would be fine. She had a good feeling about Jenna's place. Jenna had been friendly but reserved and hadn't asked a million questions about why Emily was here, what she was doing at the school, and most of all, where was her partner and Ophelia's father. Emily's chest tightened, and she pushed the thought away and blinked to stop any tears.

Augathella was going to be the right place as a temporary stop to get her head together. It couldn't be more different from Townsville. There were no balmy tropical breezes, palm trees, lush green grass, or children playing in the street outside her house. Most of all, there were no military helicopters going over as they did their daily exercises. Her breath caught and she cleared her throat before glancing over to the back. Ophelia was sitting contentedly in the baby seat, and Emily felt bad. She'd been ignoring her ever since they left the vintage tearooms.

'We are going to look at a new house for us, darling, just for a little while. Somewhere where you can play and be happy and somewhere Mummy can go to work and we'll find somebody really lovely, like a grandma, to look after you,' Emily said. In a town like this, with a mix of young people and retirees, there had to be someone who would be experienced in looking after children. Someone she could trust.

That was the next job. She slowed as she approached the third brick building along and, as Jenna had described, Emily was pleasantly surprised. Jenna's home was in a block of four units, a square brick building with a well-kept lawn greener than most of the others. The strata obviously paid for a gardener. At the edge of the lawn, there were a couple of flowering shrubs at the base of each set of steps. The units were set in a square, and the two front ones had steps back-to-back in the centre, going to front doors.

Her only worry was who else lived in the units, and she grimaced.

Beggars can't be choosers, Emily told herself. She had to take this job; it appeared the probate money wasn't going to come through very soon. She closed her eyes and took a deep breath as she parked outside the units.

CHAPTER 5

Jenna

After everyone had left, Jenna quickly wiped down the benches, turned off the coffee machine, loaded the dishwasher, and switched it on. She checked the cool room to ensure it was at the right temperature and checked the back door was locked before she took off her apron, brushed her hair, and headed down to her car at the back of the house.

Emily had been an interesting person, but she wondered if she had done the right thing by offering her the spare room in her apartment. She had assured her that the baby wasn't noisy and that she would be at work all day, and the baby would be in care. A light bulb came on in Jenna's head. Ruth Mason, Fallon's mum, would be free now that Petie Cartwright was going to kindy five days a week.

Jenna smiled to herself as she locked the front door. It hadn't taken long for her to settle into the town, and know all about who was related to who, and who fitted where.

Very different to her life on the Gold Coast where she hadn't known the name of one person in her apartment block.

Ruth had come in for coffee earlier in the week with Fallon and Callie Cartwright, and she'd been saying how bored she was.

'I'm not a gardener, the house stays tidy, and I only go out to look after this little man, the two days that Fallon is working.' She tickled her grandson under the chin. 'I've been helping Jenny get her shop ready, but I still have too much time on my hands.'

On the spur of the moment, Jenna took a left into Hill Street on her way back to her apartment. She told Emily that she'd be home around three-thirty, so she still had time before she met her there.

She smiled as she pulled up outside the house. Ruth had obviously minded Ryan while Fallon was at their meeting.

Jenna knocked on the front door, and Ruth's footsteps hurried down the hall.

'Jenna, what a surprise. How lovely to see you. Come on in, love. Fallon and I have just had a cup of tea; Ryan's due to wake up soon. The little monkey's been playing all afternoon. The pot's still warm.'

'No, thanks. Just a quick visit. I just wanted to ask you something, Ruth.'

'Sure, love, come on in.'

Jenna followed Ruth down the hall. Fallon was sitting at the table, where a pot of tea in a bright yellow and red tea cosy sat in the centre. 'Hi again, Jenna. You survived the first committee meeting, and you handled Gladys

Tingle like a pro.'

'She wasn't too bad. I was expecting worse.'

'Are you sure you don't want a cuppa?' Ruth asked.

'Thanks. I'm good. I've got somebody waiting at my apartment for me. I think I might have found someone to take Alana's room.'

'I'll have to get going, Mum.' Fallon pushed her chair back. 'I'll get Ryan and then leave you to talk to Jenna.'

'Don't rush on my account. I'll only be a minute.' Jenna stood beside the table.

'We'll be back tomorrow. I'm working again.'

Ruth beamed. 'I'll have Ryan all day. Fallon's been doing some helicopter mustering.' She pulled a face. 'I do like the idea of having my grandson to myself all day, but I would much prefer it if my daughter wasn't up in the air doing dangerous things.'

'Who are you mustering for?' Jenna asked.

'Craig Wilson's station. The other side of Braden and Callie's place. His regular guy is up in the Northern Territory, so he asked me to fill in for a couple of days.'

'Do you enjoy it?' Jenna didn't need to ask; she could see it on Fallon's face.

'I do. I've been looking forward to getting back in the air.'

'Sit down, Jenna,' Ruth said as Fallon headed up the hall.

Jenna shook her head. 'Thanks Ruth, but I can't stay long. Emily, the woman who came into the tearoom, is waiting for me to meet her at the apartment. She's starting to teach at the primary school after the holidays, Ruth, and she's got a little toddler. She's looking for someone to look after her a couple of days a week. I thought of you straight away.'

'That sounds wonderful. I'd love to meet

her.'

'Fabulous. I'll let her know. But wait until you meet her and make sure you're a fit. She seems nice and the little girl was really well behaved.'

'I appreciate you thinking of me,' Ruth said with a smile.

'My pleasure. As long as I don't turn into a Gladys Tingle, sticking my nose in.'

Ruth chuckled as they walked to the front door. 'No chance of that, love. You're a local already.'

CHAPTER 6

Amelia - the next day

Amelia Riley grabbed her hat as a gust of wind carried in gritty dust to where they waited by Ben's work car. They were parked at the aerodrome just outside of town, awaiting their visitor.

Ben was around the back, checking one of the tyres because he suspected they'd got a flat as they left their house.

'There have been a lot of kids roaming around town in the last couple of weeks, and I've heard at the council some tyres have been slashed.' He came back around shaking his head. 'No, everything is okay. It must've just been an uneven surface on the road.'

'You worry too much,' Amelia said. 'The kids in town wouldn't do that.'

Ben put his arms out and pulled her against him and turned his back to the wind to protect his wife of four weeks. He put his finger under her chin and tipped her face up to look at him.

'Are you excited about your brother coming? You've been very quiet about it.'

Amelia bit her lip and hesitated. 'I sort of don't know. It's a bit nerve-wracking because so much has changed, and it's been so long since I've seen any of my family.'

Ben's hand squeezed her shoulder gently. 'I know you're disappointed that none of them turned up for the wedding.'

'Well, that was our choice to bring it forward because of this,' she tapped her tummy, 'but I was disappointed they didn't make any effort to come. Or even to let me know they weren't coming. Not even a card or a good wish. I'm really on the outer.'

'So why do you think your brother's coming

now?'

Amelia hesitated again, not sure whether to tell Ben what she suspected Josh's mission was. She knew her family well. 'I think maybe he's at a bit of a loose end since he and Marnie split up.'

'His wife?'

'No, his girlfriend. I suspect she got sick of waiting for him to put her first. Josh is a bit like Dad. The station takes first place.'

Amelia had never been very forthcoming about her family to Ben, just that she'd moved away because her dad had been so hard. Another brother had moved away from Granite Springs at the same time and worked his own property just out of Darwin. Amelia had been surprised when Matt and Molly had got married. They had only both been nineteen, and she still remembered the argument when their father had exploded. 'She's pregnant, isn't she? She's trapped you into the marriage.'

Matt's eyes had been cold as he regarded their father. It had been the same week that Amelia had decided to pack up and leave, and she hadn't been home since.

'No, Dad,' Matt had said. 'We're getting married because we want to have a life together. We will have a family sometime, but that's not the reason that Molly and I are getting married. You can either give us your blessing, or not. It's not going to make a damn bit of difference to us.'

Amelia's enduring memory from that week was the tears that Mum had shed as two of her children had left home under difficult circumstances the same day. Circumstances totally caused by their father. Amelia had got a lift to Darwin with Matt, bought herself a van, and found a companion. Chilli Girl, the rescue dog.

Amelia had stayed very separate from the goings-on of her family after that. As she travelled through the Northern Territory and down to Queensland, meeting Ben had been the best thing for her. For the first time in her life, she felt loved for herself. Fair enough, she knew Mum loved her, but Dad was such a tyrant. He virtually told her mother how to feel and what she could express. It was a very unhealthy relationship, and sometimes Amelia wondered how she turned out normal. Or at least she thought she was normal.

'So, a loose end, you reckon?'

'Yeah, I guess Joshua just wants to see his little sister.'

The wind dropped, and Amelia reached up and took her hat off. Ben smoothed her hair. 'You are happy, though, aren't you, sweetie?'

'Happy? That's a very poor word for how I'm feeling. I have the best husband in the world, and we've only got six weeks to go until little Bump is born.' She grinned up at the man she adored. 'Or big Bump, as you called him this morning. I didn't know how to take that. I didn't know if you were having a go at my size or admiring the size of your child.'

Ben pulled her as close as he could with the big "bump" between them.

'Ouch,' she said 'Bump is kicking again.'

'Do you know he wakes me up in the night? I can feel him kicking on my side of the bed.'

'Get used to it,' she said. 'There's going to be a lot of that.'

'But you are happy, aren't you, Amelia? I know it must be hard. I see Sophie with her family, and Callie and her new brood. I know Mum is looking out for you, but it's not the same as having your own mum around for your first baby, is it?'

'Ben Riley, don't be so stupid. I'm as happy as can be, and I love your mum. She's so excited too. Anyway, I still haven't given up hope that

Mum will turn up for the birth. Maybe she's even coming with Josh today.'

The drone of an approaching aircraft reached them.

'Look, this must be Josh now.' Amelia's toes tingled with nerves as she wondered why her brother was coming now. He could've flown down from Darwin for their wedding last month. Jenny and Tom, her in-laws, had made a huge fuss of her. The Cartwright clan, as she started to think of them—Callie and Braden, and Sophie and Kent—even though Sophie was a Mason now—had made sure Ben and Amelia had the best wedding ever. Jenna had kindly given them the use of the tearooms, and it had been a small and intimate reception, but it had been the happiest day of Amelia's life.

She took a deep breath as the aircraft landed and another gust of wind puffed gritty red dirt towards them. Ben tucked his arm around her and blocked her from the wind. 'You don't want to be all dusty when your brother arrives.'

'Don't worry about it, sweetie. He's used to it.'

Her heart set up a rapid beat, and for a moment, Amelia felt faint with nerves. She clung to Ben.

'Are you okay?' he said.

'Yeah, just a bit nervous. It's been two years since I've seen any of my family. Who knows what's changed in that time? But don't worry. Josh is the normal one. It's the others who take after Dad, and that's why I got out. I really feel sorry for Mum being there with the rest of them. But Josh is a sweetie. We were the odd pair in the family, but Dad did have him under his thumb. I'm just so sad that he and Marnie aren't together anymore. But she got sick of waiting for him, I guess.'

Or putting up with Dad, she thought to

herself.

They stood there quietly as a small Cessna reached the end of the runway, and turned in to taxi towards the hangar.

Amelia's mouth dried. How ridiculous was it that she was so nervous about meeting her brother, one of her two brothers who she knew cared about her.

It seemed to take ages for the propellers to stop, and then the door opened, and her long, lanky brother jumped out of the plane. He walked across slowly, a bag slung over his shoulder, and Amelia couldn't stop herself from hurrying forward to meet him. Ben waited where they had been standing.

'Joshi,' she cried out as she opened her arms wide.

'Josh,' he said quietly, ignoring her open arms.

Amelia slowly put her arms by her side as

her brother stood there staring at her, and didn't hold his arms out for a hug. Had she so easily forgotten how closed off her family had been in terms of showing physical affection? She folded her arms over her stomach.

'It's good to see you, *Josh*,' she said. 'I was so excited when you emailed to say that you were coming to visit. How long are you going to stay?' She kept looking at him as he stared back at her. His eyes dropped to her stomach and his mouth tightened. The silence lengthened until it became awkward.

'Well, that's you here safely then,' Amelia said briskly. 'Come over and meet Ben.'

'I'll just see to the aircraft first, and then I'll meet him.' Josh put his bag down on the ground beside Amelia's feet and turned to walk back to the aircraft.

She left the bag there and walked back to Ben, tears stinging her eyes. This wasn't the Josh she knew, the Josh who she had made mud pies with, and had midnight feasts with when they were growing up. The Josh who had ridden with her, and taught her how to crack a whip. They'd been very close as children and well into their teens until he'd gone out onto the property fulltime.

Now he seemed like a totally different person.

Ben held out his hands and took both hers in his, having seen that the initial meeting hadn't gone well. 'You okay, love?'

Amelia nodded and forced her voice to stay even. 'Yes, he just has to see to the plane.'

'Okay, well, I look forward to meeting him shortly,' Ben said. Amelia sensed the hidden worry behind his response.

Well, if Josh turned out like the rest of her brothers, that was his problem. She was not going to let him make her unhappy when she had so much to look forward to, and she'd get to the bottom of why he had come to visit if it was the last thing she did.

CHAPTER 7

Jenna

Jenna was thoughtful as she drove through town. As soon as Emily left, she'd head out and see Reg.

She was generally out at the tearooms by about seven-thirty each morning. She preferred to do the baking there, and sometimes she didn't get home until after five. She'd usually have a quick shower and head off to the aged care home to see Reg.

Her grandfather had settled into a new routine. He still wandered down to the pub in the morning for half an hour, and then suss out who was heading out of town. Then he would hitch a lift with them and spend a couple of hours out with her, sitting on the front porch at the tearooms while listening to any grey nomad or tourist who wanted a chat or some information about Augathella.

At the home, Jenna would sit with him before he had his dinner. They would talk about her day, and then either play cards, read the newspaper on her phone together, or watch the quiz shows that came on before the news. Some nights they would just sit there, and Reg would hold her hand and tell her about his life as a shearer and a stockman.

'Did I tell you about the time I spent up in Western Australia?' he'd asked her last night.

'No. I thought you'd only worked around here.'

Reg tapped his nose. 'There's a lot you don't know about me yet, lassie.'

'I'm looking forward to hearing it all.'

'There's one thing I want you to know.'

'What's that?'

'I haven't got a will or anything. There was

no point. There still isn't, even though I've met your mum and you now. I haven't got anything much. When I'm gone, you'll find a shoebox in my wardrobe. In that shoebox is a little wooden box. What's in it is yours.'

Jenna had blinked away tears. 'Don't talk like that. You'll be around for years yet. You're going to give me away at my wedding when I get married.'

'Get married? Who's the lucky fella?'

She gave him a cheeky grin. 'I don't know. I'll tell you when I meet him.'

'Can't believe I got myself a daughter and a granddaughter,' he'd say each night when she left him.

'I can't believe I got myself a grandad,' Jenna said. 'Best grandad in the world, I think I've scored.'

On the way home, Jenna usually went to the pub for dinner or to pick up a takeaway and take it home. Other nights, she would catch up with the group of friends she had made in town. Kimberly from the school, Callie when she was in town, Fallon, and Amelia.

Before Alana left, they'd have dinner together one night a week. Jenna's life was busy, and she felt content. The only thing she wasn't sure about was Luke.

When she first met him on the afternoon of the opening of the tearooms a month ago, she thought he was a really nice-looking guy. They had dinner together at the pub as a group, and the group seemed to grow as more people found out that others were eating there that night. Luke walked her home, and Jenna felt the first glimmer of attraction. But that hadn't resurfaced. When he wasn't in town, she didn't miss him like she knew she would if she was attracted to him.

He was a really nice man, but there was no point in thinking about a relationship because he came from Narrabri, which might as well have been in the next continent. It was too far to drive, and his managerial job was based in Narrabri, while she had a new business and her new life in Augathella.

On the occasions he came to visit, Jenna was friendly, and they developed a solid friendship. She always suspected that underneath it all, Luke would like more.

One night, they sat and talked about it, wondering what was wrong with being friends with benefits. Maybe that wasn't far away.

***

Jenna parked in the carport, walked up the front steps and unlocked the door of the apartment. When she'd driven in, she'd seen Emily waiting. Her car was parked on the road, one door up from the units. She hurried inside and did a double check to ensure everything was as it should be. She didn't spend much time in the unit now that Alana had left.

Anyway, as she looked around the house now, everything was in its place. She had done a quick vacuum through Alana's room last weekend after Alana had collected the last of her stuff. She had barely lived there in the last six weeks as she had moved in with Rory. Jenna looked in the bathroom and the kitchen and found everything in order. When she was done, she walked back to the front door.

Emily was walking up the front steps, carrying Ophelia. Jenna hadn't had much to do with babies, but she had never seen such a well-behaved child. Ophelia looked around with her big eyes, taking everything in, snuggled into Emily, but never made a peep.

Emily was another matter. Jenna trusted first impressions, and knew Emily was a good person. She might be quiet and a bit reticent, but she was kind, and a good mother. There seemed to be a mystery behind her sudden appearance in Augathella. A teacher with no place to stay, and no one to mind her child. Jenna suspected Emily was running from something, but it wasn't her place to pry.

Anyway, Emily might find the place too small for them to stay. Jenna opened the door and held it open for Emily to walk in, carrying the wide-eyed Ophelia.

'Come on in. Sorry, the place smells a bit musty, but it's closed up all day while I'm at the tearooms. And I'm used to the Gold Coast, so I'm still not game to leave the windows open all day. Everyone says it's safe here, but you never know.'

Emily said, 'That sounds reassuring, and please don't worry about it being musty. I can't smell anything.' She stood there and looked around, Ophelia sitting on her hip, reaching up and tangling her hands in Emily's long, fair curls.

'This is lovely, Jenna. It looks fairly new.'

Jenna replied, 'Yes, I believe these units are only a couple of years old. This one has two bedrooms, and there's a little room out the back. If you decide to take it, you can choose. We can have a living area each. You could put your television out there.'

Emily shook her head. 'No need for that. I don't have a television.'

Jenna asked, 'What about furniture?'

Emily responded with a frown. 'All I have is what's in my station wagon. I'll be doing some op shopping when I find somewhere.'

Jenna gestured to the living room. 'That's a sofa that I brought from the Gold Coast when I moved here. There's really nothing in the living room at the back, because I never use it. It's sort of like a family room.'

Emily asked about the spare bedroom. 'Does it have a bed?'

'No, but that living room sofa is a sofa bed. I'm quite happy to move that into the room if that suits you. Like I said, I'm rarely here, and I have lots of other things to do once I finish at the tearooms, so I'll tell you about them later if you're interested. But we could certainly make that into a bed for you. As you can see there's no television out here. I've got a small one in my bedroom.'

'Okay,' Emily said slowly. 'I'm thinking.'

Jenna hesitated, but Emily kept talking. 'The first thing I have to do is find someone to look after missy here while I'm at school. I'm only working two days a week for the next term after the spring break next week, so I need someone quickly.'

'I hope you don't mind, but I had a bit of a brainwave after you left the tearoom this afternoon. One of my friends in town, Fallon, has a little boy, and her mum, Ruth, sometimes

78

minds him. Ruth has also been looking after one of my other friend's little boys, but Petie's now full-time at kindy and ready to go to school next year. So, Ruth's at a bit of a loose end. Anyway, I hope you don't mind, but I stopped by on my way home and asked her if she was interested in more babysitting.'

Emily's eyes brightened, and she smiled. Jenna thought, not for the first time, what a beautiful young woman she was.

Emily responded hopefully. 'What did she say? I would be more than happy to talk to her.'

'Of course, it depends on how you find her and if you're a fit. And, of course, she needs to meet Ophelia. But between you and me, I think you'd get along very well. Ruth is lovely. And very experienced. Have a think about it.'

'I will.'

'I suppose before you look for a babysitter, you need to be sure you've got somewhere to live. Come on, I'll show you the bedroom in the back area. There's a second toilet at the back of the laundry, but we would have to share a bathroom.'

'That's okay. I can stay out of your way,' Emily replied.

Jenna added, 'That'll be pretty easy because I'm not here a lot of the time. As I said, I'm generally out and about most of the day and often in the evening. Come and have a look around.'

They wandered through the apartment, and Emily exclaimed with delight when Jenna showed her the little lawn area at the back. The space was divided by a low fence from the adjacent unit.

'Oh, a garden where we can sit out and Ophelia can play.' She bit her lip again and looked hesitantly at Jenna. 'What sort of rent would you be looking at, Jenna?'

'Well, the same as Alana was paying. If

you're happy with that?'

'It depends on whether I can afford it or not. I can't pay a bond or anything until I get my first pay check at the school. Things have been a little tight since we left home.'

Jenna reassured her with a grin. 'Look, I don't require any bond. I can't imagine you're going to be any trouble. As long as you can promise no wild parties?'

Emily smiled back at her. 'No, I can't see that happening. The worst that could happen is if Ophelia got sick, she might spit up on the carpet or something, but I can buy some cleaning stuff to have just in case.'

Jenna nodded. 'Sounds like a plan. Alana was paying me a hundred dollars a week. How does that sound?'

'That's perfect.' Emily released a soft relieved sigh. 'As long as you're sure it's enough?'

'Yes, a hundred dollars a week is fair.'

'Thank you, Jenna. I accept. I wonder how soon I could meet Ruth?' Emily hitched Ophelia more comfortably onto her hip. 'It would be great to get everything organised. I had no idea it could happen so quickly, and work out so well.'

'That's the nature of this town, Emily. Everyone here is lovely and will make you feel very welcome. Now that we have your rental sorted, how would you like me to take you over to Ruth's house? You can meet her and see what you think.'

Emily asked, 'Oh really? You don't have anything else to do? It's not too late for Ruth?'

'How about this? I'll give her a call first, have a quick shower, then I'll help you bring your stuff in. After that, you can follow me over to Ruth's house, and then I'll go and visit my granddad.'

Emily nodded. 'That sounds good to me.'

'Then, how would you feel, or how would Ophelia feel, if I took you out to dinner and treated you to tea at the pub to welcome you to Augathella and my unit?'

Jenna was taken aback when she saw Emily's eyes fill with tears.

'Thank you, Jenna. You're very, very kind.' Emily shook her head. 'I might pass on dinner, but I'll certainly come to see Ruth with you.'

Jenna held out her hand to Emily and said, 'Welcome to your new home.'

CHAPTER 8

Amelia

Earlier that day

Amelia stood straight with Ben's arm around her waist as they waited for Josh to come back across the tarmac. Her stomach was in knots, and she knew it wasn't good for the baby, but she was still nervous. She had been settled in Augathella for over a year now, made so many friends, fallen in love with Ben, was about to become a mum, and had been a wife for the last four weeks.

The thought that her parents and brothers had made no effort to come down to her wedding, or even send their good wishes, or God forbid, a wedding present, was making her feel ill. She didn't really want anything from them if they hated what she had done that much.

Josh had been her biggest tormentor when they were growing up, but he had also been the brother to teach her how to ride and the one to give her a love of horses. And, if she was truthful, as much as she'd clashed with Joshua often in her later teen years, she missed him the most.

But he was the one Dad had told that Amelia was not getting any share of the property, and Josh had been the one to break it to her the night before she left. That had led to an almighty fight and lots of hurtful things said, but surely her family could accept that she was making her own life down here in Augathella.

Ben pulled her closer. 'Calm down, sweetheart, you're as tight as a bowstring. Are you feeling alright?'

'I'm sick in the tummy,' she said, 'but it's only nerves. I can't understand why Josh has come down *after* the wedding. Why couldn't they have come for the wedding? If he can come now—'

'What did the email say?' Ben had been quite surprised when there hadn't even been a phone call from Amelia's family when she had told them that they were getting married. She hadn't been able to get through on the phone so she had left a message, and followed it up with an email.

'Josh emailed. He said he was in Darwin and he'd be arriving today. That was it. I don't know whether he's going to stay with us, or at the pub. I just don't know.' Amelia's voice broke for the first time.

'I know it makes you sad, sweetie, but we've got our own family now, and we have to make Bump our priority. I don't want you getting upset, and I'll be honest, if your brother upsets you, I'll tell him where to go.'

'No, let me handle it. If there's any chance

of making peace with my family, I think this is the place to do it. This is where I can be firm. I don't care that they didn't want me working on the property. I know Dad's attitude was way out of date, and he doesn't think much of the female sex and our capability, but I still would like to have some contact with them. I don't want to be estranged. I feel sorry for Mum; she's the meat in the sandwich, but her first loyalty is to Dad, and I can understand that.'

'Okay, we'll take it step by step, and like I said, I've got your back. But if your brother says anything out of line, I'm going to say something.'

'Ben, please don't say anything until we talk about it, okay?'

'I'll think about it.'

'Promise?'

'Okay, sweetheart, I promise, but you know that I love you, and your welfare and your happiness are my priority.'

She stood and stared as Josh finished securing the aircraft and walked across the tarmac. Her eyes filled with tears as a wave of love and despair that she had lost her family filled her.

Josh looked a little bit older. The lines on his cheeks had started to deepen, and his skin was as rugged and tanned as always. But Josh had always been the best-looking of the family, and he still was. He even reminded her of Hugh Jackman sometimes, and she'd often teased him about that.

He stood in front of them, and nothing was said for a moment. Then he opened his arms. 'I'm sorry, Mellie.'

Tears flowed from Amelia's eyes as she stepped into her brother's hug. 'Oh, Josh, it's so good to see you. You had me worried before. I thought you were going to get in the plane and leave straight away.'

'And it's good to see you too. I'm sorry it's been so long.'

Amelia stayed in her brother's loving hug for a while and eventually pulled back, taking his hand. 'Joshi, this is Ben, my husband.'

Josh started to put his hand out for a handshake and paused midway, a frown on his face. 'Your husband?'

'Yes.'

'I didn't think you were getting married until November. I'm sure that's what Mum said.'

'No, we brought the date forward because,' she patted her tummy, 'we wanted to be married before the baby was born.'

'You're married?' His voice was strange. 'Already?'

'Yes, but you knew. What do you mean "already"?'

'Mum and Dad don't know. None of us

knew. You could've let us know.'

Amelia drew herself up to her full height, even though she wasn't very tall. 'Could've let you know? I emailed. And I rang. And I left messages when no one would answer their phones.'

CHAPTER 9

Amelia

The atmosphere between Ben and Josh was quite chilly, and no matter how much Amelia tried to get them chatting, she had no success. Ben tried hard at first, but Josh's response was cold and fairly non-communicative, so Ben clammed up. After their initial handshake, they walked towards his work car. Josh went to get in the back.

'No, you sit up in the front. You can see more from there,' Amelia said.

'No, no, I'm fine. I'll get in the back. You need more room, sis.'

'I thought we might go and have some lunch first before we go back to our place,' Amelia said brightly. She was getting cross at the pair of them. If they didn't want to come, they could drop her there and they could butt heads at home.

'Whatever suits you,' Ben ventured into the conversation. 'The house is a bit of a mess at the moment, Josh. We're trying to get the painting done and the new carpet down before Bump's born.'

Amelia glanced in the rearview mirror and saw the hint of a smile on her brother's face, and she relaxed a little bit. Maybe Josh was nervous about meeting Ben.

'Where do you want to go, Amelia? To the pub or the tearoom?' her husband asked.

'I think it's a bit early for the pub. Let's go to the tearoom,' she said, not mentioning she'd already booked a table. 'That way we can either have a light meal or a full meal. Whatever you want.' She slid a glance to Josh knowing what a sweet tooth he had. 'Jenna makes the best cakes, Josh.'

'Sounds good to me.' The atmosphere had

thawed a little.

As Ben drove through town and out towards the highway, Amelia half-turned in her seat. Josh was taking notice of the land around them. 'How's your work going?' she asked. 'Are you still freelancing as well as helping Dad?'

'It's okay, I suppose,' he said. 'A bit less these days. Dad is trying to give me more responsibility.' They exchanged a look, and Amelia knew her brother wasn't happy about that.

'Sounds like Dad,' she commented briefly. 'Are you still working for the same helicopter place?' she asked.

'No.'

Josh's tension had come back a little bit, and Amelia refused to let the worry take over as she turned back to the front. She put a hand on her stomach and focused on breathing evenly and deeply as Ben drove the last couple of kilometres out to the highway. He'd been quiet too.

'We're almost there,' she said. 'This is a new place in town, although I suppose it's not really in town. It's out of town. You'll meet Jenna, the girl who started it up. She only moved to town four months ago, and she's done an incredible job starting up this business. Town's becoming a lot more touristy too.' Amelia knew she was chatting for the sake of filling the silence. This was going to be a great visit if things didn't improve.

No one else spoke.

'It's a bit different from where we grew up, Josh,' she said. She caught his nod from the corner of her eye.

Ben drove into the half-full car park, and parked near the fence. Amelia went to get out, but she paused, knowing Ben would come around and help her. She still wasn't used to being almost twice her usual size.

Ellie, Jenna's young waitress, met them at the top of the steps. Amelia spoke before she could say anything about a reserved table. 'Can we go over there, Ellie?'

Ellie caught her eye and nodded. 'Sure.'

Within minutes, they were sitting around the table on the veranda.

'Nice to be almost in the bush,' Josh said. 'Not a bad place here.'

'Our house is in a similar position,' Ben ventured.

Silence again. Amelia held back a sigh.

'Yes, it appealed to both of us. It's just up the road from Ben's parents' place. We're in the last street on the other side of town and we've got an uninterrupted view across the paddocks to the hills.'

'When it came on the market, we snapped it up,' Ben said.

Josh stared at Amelia for a long moment. 'A

baby, Mellie?'

'Yes, Josh. A *husband* and a baby. Now, let's sort this out. What do you mean you didn't know we were married? Didn't Mum tell you?'

'Mum doesn't know either.'

'What? I rang and left several messages, and I emailed.' Amelia frowned.

'For the past two months, we've had no satellite. We've been totally out of touch. There was an early spring storm and it took out our satellite. Another lightning strike took out the transformer that services all the properties around us, and we've been running on generators for the past six weeks. Not only did it take out our dish but it took out all the satellite dishes within a hundred-kilometre radius, so our three neighbours are out too.'

'But surely you've been to town?' Ben asked.

Amelia looked at Ben and said, 'Town is

Borroloola and it's three hundred and fifty kilometres away from Mum and Dad's place.'

'No, we haven't been up there since before the storm. We had a downpour and a flood, and we couldn't get out and the road only cleared to the airstrip last week. I flew Mum to town last weekend and she's stocked up, ready for the wet season.'

'During the wet season, Ben, we used to get stuck there for up to six months at a time, and it was really bad. So, Mum's got a huge pantry and a huge cool room.' Amelia frowned at Josh. 'Surely you would have checked your phone messages when you got to town.'

Her brother looked sheepish. 'Would you believe we were so used to not having service, neither of us took our phones.'

'Is that the truth?'

Josh raised his voice. 'I am not a liar, Amelia.'

She looked past him. Jenna was standing at the coffee machine watching them and she raised her eyebrows at Amelia.

Amelia gave a slight shake of her head and turned back to her brother. 'So, you mean it wasn't a deliberate thing that none of the family came to our wedding?'

'I promise you, no one knew about it,' Joshua said. He shook his head slowly. 'I still can't believe my little sister is married and is having a baby. And no, we didn't know. Wait until Mum finds out. There'll be no stopping her. She misses you so much, Mellie.'

'Is the satellite working yet?'

'No, it's going to be another three weeks.'

Amelia bit her lip. 'How come you came by yourself? Why didn't Mum come with you?'

Joshua's expression turned serious. 'Mum hasn't been well. She talked about it when Dad told me to come, but she's had COVID, and she hasn't been good since she recovered.'

'Long COVID?' Amelia said, her eyes wide.

'No, she just ended up with a really bad cough afterward, and she's tired, but the last couple of weeks she's improved out of sight. She's even been back in the kitchen baking.'

'Are you sure she's alright?'

'Of course, I'm sure.'

'What did you say about Dad telling you to come? Is he alright?'

'Dad's as fit as a Mallee bull. Always has been, always will be. He's indestructible.'

'I don't know about indestructible, but I know he's immovable,' Amelia said with a grimace. 'And you didn't answer my question.'

Josh glanced over at Ben when he spoke for the first time.

'We knew you were engaged,' Josh said.

'We got engaged at our friends' Sophie and Kent's wedding.' Amelia looked affectionately at Ben. 'Ben got down on his knee beside a pot plant and proposed.'

Josh's eyes narrowed. 'And you're happy?'

'I think I have a fair idea of what's going on here,' Ben said. 'While Josh tells you the truth'—his tone held a threat— 'I'll go and get some menus.'

He stood and Amelia bit her lip as she looked across the table at her brother. 'Josh?'

'That's why I came down here. I've got to be honest, Mum did get that email, the one telling her about you and Ben getting engaged and she shared the news.'

'And what did Dad say?'

Josh shrugged. 'Same as usual, I guess. He said he didn't have to worry about you anymore. Took a load off his shoulders. Said Ben could look after you.'

Amelia made a sound between a grumble and a laugh. 'Nothing has changed, then.'

'He's alright. He's just old-fashioned. You know him, Amelia, you know what he's always been like.'

'I do, and he's lost two of his kids because of it. Mattie is over in Darwin, and I'm down here. If he had been a little bit more amenable to both of us or more reasonable, we would still be there helping out.' Her cheeks warmed as she looked across at Ben chatting to Jenna at the counter. 'But I'm pleased he did what he did because if I hadn't come down here, I wouldn't have met Ben.'

'He sent me down here, Mellie. To suss Ben out.'

Josh didn't realise that Ben had come back to the table and heard what he said.

Joshua looked from one to the other and smiled as Ben walked round the table and put his hand on Amelia's shoulder. 'You can go back and tell him I love my wife. Falling in love was the last thing I ever wanted to do, but when this feisty girl and her van turned up in town with a vicious dog—'

'Chilli Girl is not vicious,' Amelia said. She turned to Josh. 'I rescued her on the road not long after I left Darwin. You'll meet her when we go home. So, tell me, what are we going to do? How are we going to get in touch and tell Mum that we're already married and about the baby?'

'What about Matt?' Josh asked. 'Have you been talking to him? Does he know?'

'Yes, he knows. I called him at the same time I tried to call home.'

'Maybe he could drive over to the property from Darwin.'

Amelia stared at her brother as though he was crazy. 'Do you know how far that is?'

'Of course I know how far that is. You could always come home with me, Amelia. Tell them in person.'

She shook her head. 'I'm not going to risk getting stuck at the property when the baby is due.'

'How long have you got to go?'

'Five and a half weeks.' Her eyes filled with tears. 'At least I feel better now. I thought when I emailed and left a message for Mum that we were getting married and I was pregnant, I thought you'd all disowned me.'

'Don't be stupid,' Josh said.

'Surely in this day and age there's a way we can get in touch with them,' Ben said.

Josh and Amelia shook their heads at the same time.

'No, we're at the mercy of the weather, as well as the tyranny of distance,' Josh replied. He gestured outside. 'You think you're in the outback here? This is like a city compared to Granite Springs. Anyway, I'm starving, can we eat and then figure something out.'

Ben had put the laminated menus in the middle of the table and he picked one up and handed it to Josh. 'Go for it.'

By the tone of his voice, Amelia knew Ben wasn't very impressed with the first member of her family that he'd met. He reached over and squeezed her hand. 'What would you like for lunch, sweetheart?'

She shook her head. 'I'm not very hungry. Maybe just a pot of tea.'

Ben frowned at her, glared at Josh and headed to the counter.

'I guess you're ordering your own lunch, big brother.'

CHAPTER 10

Amelia

Once the ice thawed a little between Ben and her brother, conversation was civilised in the half-renovated kitchen of their sprawling home.

Amelia just sat back her in the chair at the red Laminex table that had been in the house when they bought it. She looked around; they were sitting in the kitchen instead of the living room because she was more comfortable on the kitchen chair. Ben chuckled every night when he pulled her out of the soft deep sofa that they had paid a fortune for.

Holes graced the plaster on the kitchen walls where they had pulled the original cupboards out, and taped-over electrical wires hung from every corner of the ceiling. It was a work in progress as was much of the rest of the house.

'Are you doing the work yourself, Ben?' Josh asked as Ben walked in from feeding Chilli Girl.

'As much as I can, but there's not a lot of time for the house at the moment. I've been working a fair bit of overtime at the shire.'

'Maybe I can earn my board this week and give you a hand? Happy to.'

Ben nodded, and Amelia was pleased to see that an olive branch had been offered.

Ben pulled out a chair, and Joshua put his hands on the table in front of him. His voice was gentle. 'Don't get cross, Mellie, but I think we need to clear the air.'

'We do,' she agreed.

'This is the last thing I ever would've expected you to do. I thought you wanted to have a career as a stockwoman. Now look at you, hitched, having a baby, and making your own love nest.'

Ben made a snorting sound but left it to Amelia to answer.

'Yes, I'm pregnant, I'm married, and I'm making a home. Thank you very much, Joshua,' Amelia replied.

He grinned. There'd been no malice in his words, and Amelia knew it was just Joshua's way of getting to the point. He was direct.

Ben sensed that they would be better off alone, so he picked up his keys when he finished the coffee Amelia had made while he was out feeding Chilli. 'Braden called when I was out the back. He asked if I had the time to go out and have a look at something on his place this afternoon. Are you two right here by yourselves? You won't kill each other, will you?' Ben said with a grin.

'We're fine. We've been fighting for as long as I can remember and we've both survived,'

Josh said.

'What's this "something" you've got to look at?' Amelia tipped her head to the side. She appreciated Ben's concern for her, and she knew that he must trust Josh if he was going out to give them space. 'You don't have to go, sweetheart. Perhaps it's a beer Braden wants you to look at?' Her smile was wide.

'No, seriously, Braden's putting in more dongas for the cattle crew and he wants me to check out the best location with regard to the water supply. I'm sure there'll be a beer involved at the end.' Ben turned to Joshua. 'I'm a building inspector in Charleville. I took some flex-leave to meet you, but I don't mind going out to help Braden.'

'What do you two want to do for dinner? How about we go out to the pub when you get back?' Amelia suggested.

Ben nodded. 'Sounds good to me. We'll take

Josh out and show him the sights of Augathella.'

'Well, it's certainly more cosmopolitan than our place,' Josh said.

Ben raised his eyebrows. 'Can't wait to visit one day.'

'And we will, Ben. Once the baby's born, and you get some leave from the Shire, we'll drive up and see Mum and Dad, because I think if I wait for them to come down here, I'll be waiting for a long time.'

'Oh, I don't know about that,' Josh said. 'Mum is keen to see you. She just wasn't sure how long you'd stay here. My sister's not the best communicator, Ben,' Josh explained. 'We didn't know you were a local here and my sister was putting roots down.'

'She is.' Ben bent down and kissed Amelia. 'I'll make a booking at the pub for dinner on the way through town.'

'Now, Josh,' Amelia said when the front

door closed behind Ben. She waited until she heard his car back out of the car port. 'Tell me what you're really doing here.'

'I told you. I came to check out your fiancé, and then I rock up and find out you're already married.'

'Obviously the communication issue we've discovered. You could've saved yourself a trip. You could have taken your phone to town, or you could have called me from Darwin. None of it is my fault, Josh.

'Anyway, no matter how much you and Dad don't like that I'm here, and I'm married, and I'm pregnant, there won't be any changes. I love Ben; he's a good man, and we are going to make a good life together. You and the family have to accept that. I'm a big girl now, and capable of making my own life decisions.'

'He seems okay,' Josh finally said.

'He's more than okay. And I love him, and I

love his parents. I've settled into this town, made some great friends, and I'm happy here.'

'I can tell. But what about not working with cattle and working on the land? That's all you ever wanted to do at home. Remember, you just wanted to be out there.'

'Well, that was really all I knew, wasn't it, Josh? I wanted what Dad wouldn't agree to but I found another path for my life.'

'Okay, I guess I can accept that.'

'You have to. Tell me, has Dad made it up with Matt?'

'No, we never hear from them.'

'I wish I was there to sort it out.'

Josh reached over and put his hand on Amelia's. 'You never change, Mellie. You always liked everyone to get along, and you always want to see everyone happy. I think it's the trait I love in you the most.'

Amelia's eyes pricked as she thought of the

good times she'd had growing up at Granite Springs. 'Yep, I did like everyone to be happy.'

'And the old man really let you down, didn't he?'

'He surely did.'

'Mum was devastated when you took off and bought that van. The first time you sent a photo, I thought she was going to have a conniption.'

'Well, it worked out really well. I met some lovely people on the road, had some great experiences, and ended up in the best town in Australia.'

'Okay, sounds good to me.' Josh lifted his hand and covered his mouth as he yawned. 'Do you mind if I go and have a bit of a kip? What time is it now?'

'It's just after three. I'll show you the guest room. That was the second room we did up, after the nursery. I might go and have a rest, and then we'll take you out on the town tonight.' Amelia stood and gathered their cups and carried them over to the sink. She turned around, surprised to find her brother standing behind her.

Joshua reached out and pulled her into a hug. 'You know, I really have missed you, Mellie. We all have.'

CHAPTER 11

Jenna

Jenna sat on the double sofa in Ruth's family room and watched the interaction between Emily and Ruth. Ruth was such a lovely person; always smiling and happy. As soon as they walked in, she extended her arms for Ophelia to come and snuggle in with a giggle and a smile.

Emily's eyes had widened slightly, and then she smiled. 'Hello, Ruth, it's lovely to meet you, and you certainly have the touch.'

'What a gorgeous little girl,' Ruth said, holding out one hand to Emily and shaking it not in a masculine way, but with affection. 'It's lovely to meet you, Emily, and I'm so pleased you've come to town. I think you'll fit in very well at the school. And your timing couldn't have been better. Jenna probably told you that

I've been babysitting on and off for the last year or so, and my last little man is about to start school full-time next year. He'll be at kindy full-time next term, so apart from helping out our daughter with her little boy a couple of days a week, I'll be at a loose end, so if you are happy with what you see here, I'll be happy to work out which days with you.'

'Thank you for welcoming me to your home, Ruth.'

Jenna looked up as Fallon came in carrying Ryan, wrapped in a towel

'I'm still here. I decided to give Ryan his tea and his bath. Saves our tank water at home.' She looked across at Emily. 'Hi, I'm Fallon. You must be Emily. Welcome to town.' She turned and looked at her mother and the toddler in her arms. 'What a gorgeous little girl.'

Ruth offered the ever-ready cup of tea and Jenna was surprised when Emily accepted.

'Thank you, just black, no sugar.'

Even though it was late in the afternoon and closer to dinner time, Ruth brought out a tray of homemade biscuits.

As far as Jenna knew, Emily hadn't eaten since she'd first arrived at the teashop. She'd had a couple of cups of coffee there, and hadn't eaten at the apartment. She almost looked fragile, and with her various comments about money, Jenna wondered whether she was saving money on not eating as she should. She'd keep an eye on that.

She walked to the door. 'I'm off to see Reg now. You're right to get in at home, Emily?'

Emily patted her pocket. 'Yes, I've still got the key.'

'And if you change your mind about dinner, I'd love to see you there.'

'Are you having dinner at the pub?' Fallon asked.

Jenna replied, 'Yes, I usually go there after I

leave Reg. I guess I'm lazy. The last thing I feel like doing after being at the tearooms all day is cooking for myself.'

'Jon and I were thinking about going there tonight. That's why I gave Ryan his tea early. Jon needs to go to the rural store if he can get into town before it closes.'

'Sounds good. It would be nice to have a get together. Emily, think about coming for dinner because Callie and Braden are coming into town too, Jon said. Callie works at the primary school. Have you been there yet? Have you met anyone?'

Emily hesitated, and Jenna chimed in, repeating her earlier offer. 'Emily, if you'd like to come, I'd like to treat you to welcome you as my new tenant and to welcome you to town. Give it some thought. If you do decide to come, I'll be there about six.'

Jenna stood and went to carry her cup into

the kitchen, but Ruth waved her away, saying, 'Leave it on the tray, sweetie. I'll sort that out.'

'We will see you at the pub, Ruth?' Jenna asked.

'No, I want to watch that music show on TV tonight. It's getting close to the finals.'

Jenna chuckled and headed out to her car.

CHAPTER 12

Emily

Emily was surprised by how comfortable she felt in Ruth's home. In fact, she was surprised at how comfortable she had felt since arriving in Augathella this morning. For some reason, it just felt right. Ophelia had been so well-behaved, not that she was usually anything else, and everyone had been so welcoming.

As she walked out the door after negotiating a very reasonable rate with Ruth for babysitting Ophelia, she held her arms out to the little girl.

'Mum, mum,' she yelled loudly. 'Din din?'

'If you'd like to go out for tea, I'm more than happy for you to leave Ophelia here for a couple of hours,' Ruth offered. 'It's almost six now.' Ruth took Emily's hand again. 'It's been so lovely to meet you, Emily. I hope you enjoy living in Augathella. Jenna is a sweetheart, and she'll make a great landlady.'

'I already feel as though she's more a friend,' Emily replied. 'I'm actually overwhelmed by the welcome I've had, and how everything has worked out in one day.'

'Well, if you want to finish off the day with dinner at the pub, the offer is there.'

Emily's eyes welled with tears. Maybe things are going to look up a bit, she thought to herself. Her welcome had been warm and comforting. Not one person had asked difficult questions or wanted to know her background or why she was here, and that made her feel safe.

'Thank you, Ruth. I will accept your kind offer. I'll take Ophelia home and give her a bath and tea, and I'll get the porta cot.'

Ruth waved a hand. 'No need, love. There's a nursery with a cot and a bed in the spare room. And lots of toys for all ages.'

Emily had surprised herself. A week ago, a month ago, a year ago, going out in a group and leaving Ophelia behind would have been the last thing she considered.

The last thing she'd have been able to do.

##

Emily drove back the two streets to their new home and carried Ophelia inside. She held her daughter in one arm and went inside and sat her on the floor with a couple of toys. 'You stay there. I'll be back in a minute. I've just got to get our food out of the fridge, sweetie.'

Ophelia smiled at her and picked up her favourite toy, a little yellow car with one missing wheel.

It only took a couple of minutes for her to empty out the camp fridge. She smiled as she opened the fridge in the kitchen. Jenna had already cleared the bottom two shelves for her, as she said she would, and one of the drawers in the freezer was empty. She didn't have anything frozen to put in there yet. Once she had the food stored, Emily brought Ophelia into the kitchen and sat her on the floor, putting out more toys from her bag.

Emily smiled as she handed the toys over. They carried all their belongings with them in the car—she had no intention of ever going back to Townsville—their clothes and their bedding, and the food filled the back of the station wagon, but toys certainly made up the majority of their luggage.

She quickly peeled a potato and chopped off a piece of pumpkin to prepare the mash for Ophelia's dinner. There was one piece of chicken left from last night, and she sliced it up into bite-sized pieces. Once the vegetables were cooked, she mashed them with some butter and milk. She sat at the table with Ophelia on her lap; her little girl was still too little to sit in a chair, and they didn't have any small chairs with them because there wasn't enough room in the station wagon. She'd have to think about it; perhaps if she had enough money to top the car up, she could drive down to Charleville and look at some op shops. Once the tank was full, she'd be using very little fuel in this small town.

Ophelia was well-behaved. She ate all of the food that Emily offered to her. After she was finished, Emily wiped her face and hands with a wet flannel washer. 'I think, if we're in luck, there is one little container of jelly and fruit left in our bag. Let's have a look, shall we?'

Ophelia started pointing as soon as Emily mentioned the jelly. Her daughter had a sweet tooth and had enjoyed the one biscuit that Emily allowed her to have at Ruth's house.

After she cleaned up in the kitchen, she

carried Ophelia into the bathroom and ran a shallow bath. Ophelia splashed, and eventually Emily lifted her out, nuzzling her nose into her baby's warm, sweet-smelling skin.

She grimaced as she dried Ophelia, embarrassed to see how threadbare the towel was. It would be wonderful to get a pay packet, and be able to replace some of their linen.

'Yes, definitely a trip to the op shop tomorrow. There's nothing else we need to spend money on until my first pay. New towels, and maybe some new clothes for you.'

Ophelia was wide awake, giggling, and playful. 'Out,' she said, pointing to the door.

'Do you want to go outside, sweetie? We'll go out and have a quick look in the back garden before we go back to Ruth's.'

Emily carried her daughter out the back door and sat on the steps, her eyes fixed on the horizon. Her stomach growled, and she realised how hungry she was. She knew she had to eat more; she had to stay well to look after Ophelia, because if she got sick, there was nobody else.

Once the sun had slipped below the horizon and lit up the evening sky in a palette of apricots and mauves, Emily held Ophelia's hand and helped her walk up the back steps and through the door. Ophelia walked around the lounge and sat back down on the blanket where her toys were.

Emily walked across to her bag and took out her purse and opened it. The fuel docket from today fluttered to the floor, and she picked it up and put it safely in the back. She needed to keep track of her money because everything she did was in cash.

She opened the zipper at the back part of her wallet and pulled out the bundle of notes, counting what she had. She still had four hundred and fifty dollars left, which would fill the car up, buy food for the next couple of weeks, and once she'd paid two weeks rent to Jenna, it would leave her a little to spend at the op shop. Perhaps she could look for a small highchair, and when they finished here, she could take it back. She certainly had enough to buy a cheap meal at the hotel. Jenna's invitation had been kind, although she wouldn't let Jenna pay for her dinner.

Without thinking about what she was doing, she put the money safely back in the second part of her purse and slipped twenty-five dollars into the front section. She would go out for dinner, and have an entrée only. It would be good to meet people from the school before she started work.

Emily still wondered whether she had done the wrong thing taking this job and stopping here in Augathella; perhaps she should have just kept heading for South Australia. But the opportunity of having a term's work and getting some money behind her had been enticing. The only problem was, it was a lot closer to Narrabri than Townsville had been. However, there was no way she would go that way; she would stick to the far western highway.

For the first time in a long time, contentment stole over her as she sat there, watching her little girl playing happily with her toys.

CHAPTER 13

Jenna

Jenna was surprised but happy to see Emily walk through the side door of the pub; Emily stood hesitantly looking around.

'Emily,' she called. 'Over here.'

Emily looked over and Jenna gestured to the table where she was sitting with two other couples. Two young boys were bickering at the other end of the table, and the noise was so loud that one of the women turned around and said, 'If you boys don't stop squabbling, you will be sitting outside.' There was immediate silence, and to Emily's surprise, the boys settled down. Jenna stood up and walked over to stand beside Emily.

'Emily, this is Callie and Braden Cartwright, and Sophie and Ben Mason.' The men stood up and nodded to her, and the two women smiled their welcome.

'Welcome, Emily. I'm Callie. I believe you're joining us at the primary school after the holidays.'

'Yes, I am,' Emily said. 'It's nice to meet you all.' The man sitting beside Callie stood and came round, pulling out a chair for her.

'So, you've moved to Augathella to start work at our lovely school,' the other woman, Sophie, said.

'Yes,' Emily said, 'I've heard good things about the school.'

'Very different to when Braden, Kent, and I went there. It was only a two-teacher school back in the dark ages.' Sophie grinned. 'Braden and I are brother and sister; in case you were wondering.'

Emily's gaze dropped down to Sophie's stomach; she was obviously very pregnant and

129

looked like she didn't have long to go. For the first time, she also noticed the double pram against the wall behind Callie. 'Yes, I'm looking forward to working there. When is your baby due?' she asked.

'Six weeks,' Sophie replied, 'but it feels like six months. This has been the longest pregnancy on earth.'

Callie laughed. 'For goodness' sake, Sophie, you were four months pregnant before you found out you were even having a baby.'

'You know me, Cal, I like to whinge,' Sophie said. But she was a pretty girl, and her smile was wide. Emily felt as welcome here as she was at Ruth's house, and by Jenna at both the cafe and in her apartment. The feeling of contentment that had settled in her through the day stayed with her. The conversation was fast, and she was happy enough to sit back and listen to the bantering between Sophie and Braden and their partners.

A little boy walked up to Emily. 'Hello, my name is Petie. What's your name?'

Emily said gently. 'Hello, Petie, I'm Emily.'

'That's a pretty name,' Petie said.

'Those two naughty boys down there are my brothers,' Petie explained. 'That's Rory and Nigel, and they are arguing again. Mummy said if they wake the twins up again, they are in big trouble. I know how to be quiet.'

Braden glanced down to the back end of the table and leaned over to Callie. 'Don't worry, love, I'm keeping an eye on them.'

'Twins?' Emily asked him with a smile.

'Yes, a big surprise for us when they made their appearance very quickly.' Braden leaned over the table as the noise in the bistro was getting louder. 'Jenna tells us you have a little girl. How old is she?'

'Eighteen months.'

'Shall we go and order?' Jenna interrupted. 'Before it gets too busy. I'm going to get some menus, Emily, and you can tell me what you'd like.'

Emily shook her head. 'No, I'll come with you. I'm not going to let you pay for my dinner. You've been way too kind to me today already. I should pay for your dinner.'

Jenna shook her head. 'No, it's my shout. You can buy me a drink if you like, though. I'll have a white wine.'

'Okay, thank you. Sounds good to me.'

'I'll go and get the drinks,' Kent said. He stood. 'A lemon squash for Callie and Sophie, a beer for Braden, and a wine for Jenna. What would you like Emily?'

'Just a squash for me too. Thank you, Kent.'

Braden walked to the bar with Kent, and Emily spoke to Callie. 'How old are your twins?'

'Just gone six months,' she replied. 'Petie,

Nigel, and Rory are my stepsons, and now we have Meggie and Munro.'

'Twins would be a handful,' Emily said.

Callie nodded. 'You could say that, but I'm back at work one day a week, and Braden stays in with the twins that day.'

'He's a good dad to do that,' Emily said, and as soon as the words came out of her mouth, a wave of depression hit her. She sat rigid, wanting to flee the room, and go—

Where?

There was nowhere to go. Augathella was as good a place as any, but staying here too long would lead to questions; questions that she didn't want to answer. She closed her eyes and concentrated on listening to the sounds in the room as the clinical psychologist had taught her.

Don't get too close, she told herself.

CHAPTER 14

Jenna

Jenna smiled as she spotted Amelia walk in.

'Look. There's Amelia and Ben. Is everyone happy if we invite them to join us?'

Of course,' Sophie replied and the others nodded. 'That must be her brother who was coming to visit. She mentioned that at our meeting yesterday.'

Jenna glanced across at Emily, who seemed to have lost her colour in the last little while and hadn't spoken for a few minutes.

'Emily, are you okay?' Jenna asked. Emily nodded without speaking, and Jenna worried that someone might have said something to offend her. 'Is there something wrong?' she asked quietly.

Emily shook her head. 'Just a bit tired.'

'It won't be a late night,' Jenna said sympathetically. 'You've had a big drive today.'

'Okay, I'll give them a wave.' Sophie's voice interrupted their conversation. 'There are three spare chairs at the end of the table down beside the kids.'

Soon, Amelia and Ben had joined them. Amelia introduced her brother before they sat down. 'Everyone, this is Josh. Josh, this is Braden and Callie, and on the other side, Sophie and Kent, and this is Jenna. You'll remember her from lunch.'

She looked at Emily, and Jenna stepped in. 'Hi, guys. Welcome, Josh. This is Emily, a new teacher at the school next term.'

Jenna glanced across at Emily as she nodded briefly to Amelia, Ben, and Josh, and then put her head down again. She was very pale, and Sophie looked at Jenna and raised her eyebrows.

Jenna gave her a slight nod to acknowledge

her concern as Amelia's brother pulled out a chair beside Jenna.

'Okay if I sit here?' he asked.

Jenna nodded, and although she was more focused on Emily, she wondered what Amelia's brother was like.

So far, he'd seemed okay, although she had been aware of some tension at the table when they'd had lunch at the tearooms today.

As Josh settled at the table, and told Ben he'd like a beer when asked, Jenna kept one eye on Emily, but it was almost as though Emily was elsewhere in her thoughts, looking down and seemingly unaware of the room around her.

The conversation at the table ceased for a moment, and gradually, Emily looked up, becoming aware of the silence.

She smiled, but to Jenna it seemed forced, and gradually, some colour returned to her cheeks. 'Sorry if I zoned out for a minute. I am tired after the big drive today. It will be good to be settled.'

The conversations picked up again, and Jenna was pleased to see Emily respond to Sophie.

Josh turned to Jenna and asked, 'So, Jenna, tell me what you are doing in Augathella. Amelia said the tearooms belong to you. Nice lunch today. How long have you been here?'

Jenna replied, 'Not long, probably about three or four months now.'

'And are you liking living here?'

'I'm loving living here,' she said, 'It's a great little town. The business is going well, and I've made great friends.'

'Where are you from?' His voice was deep and as she met his gaze, a slow spark fired. She hadn't realised what a good-looking guy he was until she'd really looked at him.

'City. Country living is new to me. How

about you?' His blue-eyed gaze held hers and it was hard to look away.

'I'm from a place called Granite Springs, where Amelia grew up. I don't know if she's mentioned it.'

Jenna had heard a little bit about Amelia's background and knew that she had left home because of some issues with her parents.

'That's up in the Northern Territory, isn't it?'

'It's pretty much on the border between Queensland and the Northern Territory at the base of the Gulf. We've got a big spread, and I work it with our dad.'

'I grew up in Brisbane, worked on the Gold Coast for a while, and came from there to here.'

'A bit of a change,' Josh said. 'But one for the better. Are you here to stay or is it just a business stop?'

'No, I think I'll most probably stay on. I'm

really starting to like the town. But who can really say? Who knows what's around the corner?' she said.

'Ha, sounds like there's man on the scene,' he said with a grin.

Jenna burred up. 'Why would a man on the scene make a difference to whether I want to stay or go?'

He lifted both hands and put them up. 'Sorry, sorry, obviously a sensitive point.'

'No, not a sensitive point at all. Don't you think that a woman is able to decide what she wants to do, irrespective of whether a man is involved or not? For example, I'm settled here. I've got a good business going, so if I went to the Gold Coast and I met someone I wanted to have a future with, I'd expect *him* to follow me here. I don't see why the woman always has to follow the man.'

'I'm sorry, I didn't mean to step on your

toes.'

'And how about any relationship up there with you?' He'd really pushed Jenna's buttons. 'Is that why you're staying at Granite Springs, because you've met the love of your life there?'

'I'm way too busy for that sort of thing in my life.' A glimmer of temper laced his voice. 'Dad and I run almost half a million acres; it keeps us pretty busy.'

Jenna shrugged.

Josh shook his head slowly. 'Look, I don't know how we got into this conversation, but I don't understand what we were arguing about.'

'We're not arguing. We are having a discussion. Excuse me, I need to speak to Sophie.'

***

Joshua watched Jenna walk around the table. She was a very pretty woman with a determined step and he let his gaze take her in as she stood

140

behind Sophie and put her hand on her shoulder. As she did, she looked back at Josh, whose eyes were still on her. Despite their lively conversation—almost an argument—attraction surged as he'd sat beside her. Josh had actually noticed Jenna as soon as they'd walked in. She had presence, her smile was happy and she held herself confidently. Plus, she was a very attractive woman.

He wasn't going to look away, and she held his gaze as if they were sharing the same thoughts. She seemed interested and determined in what she was doing, and he couldn't help but admire her. It didn't hurt that she had beautiful eyes, a lovely shade of green. A tingle ran down his back and from that moment, his heart raced as a connection established. Josh had never felt this way before.

He sat there for a moment until he looked away, then glanced up to the end of the table, where Ben had his arm around Amelia, and their heads were touching. He had come here to check if Ben was the right person for Amelia, on Dad's instructions of course, and he wondered why he had so readily agreed.

They were happy, but even if Amelia had chosen someone else, it had nothing to do with him or Dad. His sister had always known what she wanted and had gone for it. It was just a shame that Dad held such old-fashioned values about a woman's place.

Josh was proud of Amelia for sticking to her guns and leaving home. It looked like she had found herself a good home and, from what he had observed so far, a good man who obviously loved her.

Just to make sure, he'd stay a couple of weeks. While he was here, he'd have a look around because he had often thought of buying some land for himself. He liked the look of the land he'd seen as he'd flown in.

Where did he fit into the property with Dad? He was uncomfortable with the family dynamic Dad had created over the past few years. Amelia and Matt had gone, and as for his other brothers, they seemed quite happy, married, and settled in houses a hundred kilometres away from the main house, looking after their sections of the station. They rarely came back to the main homestead. Dad's three-monthly meetings were about the only time they saw Peter and Robert.

Josh sat back and looked at the happy interaction around him, his eyes occasionally straying to Jenna as she worked her way along the table and spoke to everyone. This was something that was totally out of his experience. Families and the rare social occasions had never held this warmth or happiness.

Josh folded his arms and leaned back in his chair. He was in his early thirties and still living in the same house with his parents; he had never lived anywhere else.

Ben had told him that Braden had quite a spread a few kilometres out of Augathella. He'd have a talk with him and see if anything was on the market. It wouldn't hurt to have something down here; it would be close to Amelia for visits, and he could put a manager on the place.

And more importantly, it would be mine, he thought.

CHAPTER 15

Joshua

Josh was still in Augathella a week later. He had been out to Braden Cartwright's property a few times and had been really interested to see the way they did things out here. He and Braden had really hit it off, and Josh was enjoying sitting out there having a beer with him this afternoon. The weather was starting to warm up now.

'I'll have to start getting things done before the heat arrives. I've fallen behind over the past six months since the twins arrived, and now that Callie's gone back to work, there doesn't seem to be enough days in the week. How warm does it get up your way?'

'We're a lot warmer than this through the day, even in the winter,' Josh said, thinking of the hot days and cool nights he'd left at home.

'I'm used to the heat in the summer, having grown up with it. It's when it's wet and we're flooded in, can't get out to the cattle, that's a problem. We've had unseasonable floods this winter, and that's caused a myriad of problems too. Couldn't even get to the airstrip. We lost our satellite relay and because of that it caused a few problems between Amelia and me. I came down here to suss Ben out before they got married,' he said with a grin. 'And when I turned up here, not only are they already married but they're having a baby,' he added.

'You didn't know?' Braden asked.

'No, and my parents don't know either, so I'll be telling them when I go back. Amelia would prefer to tell them face-to-face now that she's learned what happened with the satellite and the phones, but it's impossible. She can't travel. Maybe when I go up, I can talk Mum into coming down here,' Josh explained.

'Don't worry yourself about Ben. He's a good bloke. I've known him all my life, and he'll look after your sister.'

'Yes, I'm starting to figure that out myself. I really like the country down here, and the people,' Josh admitted.

'It might tempt you to move down here,' Braden said.

'Actually, that's what I've been sussing out. I'm looking for some land just to diversify a bit and be a bit independent. You know, something of my own instead of the family stuff. Do you know of anything for sale at the moment?'

'I know a couple of places coming up. I don't know how much land you're looking at or how much you want to spend, but I can introduce you to some people,' Brayden offered.

'Sounds good. I'll give you my email, and we'll keep in touch,' Josh said as Braden's two oldest boys walked into the shed.

'Mum said dinner's ready,' one of the boys announced.

'I'll get going,' Josh said.

'No, come on in. Callie said that she was hoping you'd stay. She's cooked enough.' Braden replied.

'Thanks, Braden, you've made me very welcome,' Josh said.

'It's the country. You should know how things are done,' Braden responded.

Josh shook his head. 'It's very different where we are. No local pub to go to, no one lives within two hundred kilometres of us. A totally different way of life.'

'I can sort of understand now why Amelia is happy here,' Josh mused. 'She loved the place as much as I do, but Dad wouldn't have her out on the cattle. Now she's living in town and seems as happy as anything.'

'She did some work for me before she and

Ben first hooked up. In fact, she met Ben out here one day when that dog of hers bit Ben.' Braden chuckled.

'Yeah, I've heard the story about Chilli Girl,' Josh said with a smile.

'Don't worry, she's happy. Come on, we'll see what Callie's cooked up for us,' Braden suggested.

CHAPTER 16

Jenna

The next night

'Thanks for coming out with me, Jenna,' Josh said.

Jenna nodded. 'I enjoy eating out at the pub. Saves me cooking.'

'I thought it would give Ben and Amelia some space. I've been in the house with them a week now, and it's not a real big place.'

'So, it wasn't the attraction of my company?' Her eyes met Josh's squarely.

'Yes, it was. I enjoyed spending time with you at the pub the other night, so I thought if the two of us had some time together, we could have a chat. Get to know each other.'

'What did you want to have a chat about?'

'Get to know you? Find out a bit more about

the town, the people in it, and how much you like
it.'

'I like it.'

'Amelia said she worked for you for a
while.'

'Yes, she helped me when we were starting
out and during the grand opening; we had it a
couple of months ago.'

'What about Ben? Do you know him very
well?'

Disappointment flooded though Jenna.
She'd been really excited when Josh had got her
number from Amelia and called her a couple of
days ago to ask her out.

'Is that why you asked me out? To snoop
around about your new brother-in-law? That's
pretty low.'

'If I'm honest, yes, I do want to know more
about Ben. I like him, but my sister is important
to me. I want to go home knowing she's happy.'

Jenna folded her arms. 'Ask her.'

'I have. But to be honest, that's not the reason I asked you out.'

'Well, even if I did know Ben very well, I wouldn't feel comfortable talking about him. But luckily for me, I don't know him very well, so I won't be telling any secrets. But I can tell you he's highly regarded in the community, and that's all I'll say. Now, perhaps we can order, eat, and I can go home.'

'Oh, come on, Jen. Don't be like that.'

'Like what? I feel like I've been made use of, to be taken out for dinner so you can find out the gossip about your brother-in-law. I think that's a pretty low act, Joshua.'

Josh leaned back in his chair, ran his hand through his hair.

Despite her anger, Jenna still appreciated how good looking he was, and other than the Ben stuff, she found his company enjoyable. Josh was interesting, and she'd enjoyed listening to his stories about where he and Amelia had grown up. In fact, more than enjoyable, she really had felt that spark that was missing with Luke, and that's why she'd been so cross when she thought he had only asked her out to pry about Ben.

'Okay, truce.' Their eyes met and held, and a warm quiver shot down her back. 'Tell me some more about where you live. I thought Augathella was isolated and small, but it sounds like you have a totally different lifestyle up there.'

'We do, but tell me some more about you. I've been talking about home since we got here. What about you? You grew up in the city, you said.'

'Yes, Brisbane. Then when I moved to the Gold Coast I got into real estate, and that filled in a few years. I got jaded. I bought an old house and started a business out here.'

'But what did you do in real estate? It's a bit different to making cups of tea for tourists.'

'Hey, it's more than that.' Jenna leaned forward, and her arm brushed Josh's. Heat ran up her arm and she looked down at his skin with surprise. Desire followed quickly, and her cheeks warmed as her thoughts turned in that direction. 'I'm quite an entrepreneur and businesswoman if you must know.' She forced a chuckle as her gaze stayed on Josh and she tried to ignore the feelings that were running rampant in her body.

Josh nodded and smiled at her. 'I can see that. I've heard nothing but positive comments about your venture out there. Apparently, it's the talk of the district.'

'I'm pretty happy out there. And I don't know if Amelia's mentioned it, but the upside to coming to town was that I discovered that my grandfather, who I hadn't known about, was living out here.'

'Go on, really?'

'Yeah, really.'

'And it was just a coincidence that you encountered him?'

'It was meant to be, I guess, if you believe in that sort of thing. Have you ever been to the pub in the morning?' she asked.

Josh grinned. 'No, why would I be at the pub before lunch? A bit early for a beer.'

'Have you driven past?'

'Yeah, I probably have if I think about it.'

'Well, my grandad sits in the chair at the door from opening time. He's a local identity.'

'You're talking about Reg.'

'Yep, Reg is my grandad.'

'I was walking down the street yesterday to go to the butcher for Amelia, and he called me from across the road, waylaid me, wanted to know who I was, what I was doing in town, who

I was related to and how long I was staying. We had quite a good chat. When I told him where I came from, he made me pull up another chair, and we chatted for about half an hour. When he heard I was from the north, he told me about some trips he'd done when he was young. He told me about his new daughter and granddaughter, but I didn't know it was you. He's quite the character.'

A warm feeling suffused Jenna's chest. 'He is a sweetie.'

'He told me they call him Reg, the fella from Augathella. Love it.' Josh reached across the table and took Jenna's hand. 'Pretty special to discover your family.'

'Should we go and order now?' she said as that damn blush rose up into her cheeks again. Her whole body was on fire.

'Would you like another wine?' Josh asked.

Jenna looked at her glass and nodded. 'Why

not? I'm walking home.'

The rest of the evening was very pleasant, and she had quickly forgiven Josh for his interrogation about Ben.

As they stepped out of the pub, it was bright outside. The full moon had risen, and the beautiful, fat yellow orb hung low over the paddocks to the east.

'Beautiful, isn't it?' she said as Josh took her hand.

'Sure is. You should see it up our way, The Milky Way sky is absolutely incredible.'

They were quiet as they walked down the street to her front gate, and Jenna turned to him when they stopped outside.

For the first time in a week, she regretted that Emily and Ophelia were sharing her apartment. She would have invited Josh in for a coffee, but didn't want to disturb them. She didn't want the night to end. It was a new feeling for her, and one that she was going to examine later.

'Thank you so much for taking me out, Josh. I ended up enjoying the night.'

'So did I. Maybe we can do it again before I leave.'

'Sounds like a plan.'

He reached down and kissed her cheek, smiled, and went to turn away.

Jenna put her hand to her cheek, but before she could think, Josh turned around and put his arms around her.

'Is it okay if I kiss you good night properly?'

Her eyes were wide as she nodded, and the full moon was soon blotted out by Josh's head as Jenna was thoroughly kissed goodnight. His lips were warm on hers, and softer than she'd imagined. It had been a long time since she had been kissed like that. Actually, she had never been kissed like that before. And she didn't want it to end. Josh's hands were on her waist and her skin was burning there too.

'See you tomorrow?' he whispered as he lifted his head.

'Yes, please.'

'What time do you open?'

'I get there about seven-thirty if you'd like an early breakfast.'

'See you in the morning.'

Josh was whistling happily as he walked back to the corner.

Jenna stood with her hand on her lips until he disappeared. At last, she knew what the spark was everyone was talking about. It had taken a while to experience, but wow.

CHAPTER 17

Emily

The first week that Emily had shared the unit with Jenna had gone by very quickly for her. Jenna had been extra busy at the tearoom and had left before Emily was awake the last three days. On the rare occasion that they were in the house at the same time, Jenna hadn't stopped smiling.

Emily had been to the primary school on the last day of term, and Callie had taken her under her wing. She had also taken Ophelia to Ruth's place on two mornings to give Ophelia a chance to settle. She'd been a bit put out that her little girl had waved her off from Ruth's arms as Emily backed out of the driveway.

Ophelia had been settled when she picked her up. 'Happy as anything. I don't think she even missed me,' Emily said to Ruth.

'And school was good?' Ruth asked. 'What you were hoping for?'

'Yes, it was. Even better, the principal asked me if I could do three days because someone else dropped out, but I said I couldn't commit until I checked with you.'

'I'd love to, and if it clashes with Ryan's days, Fallon can drop him here because she has to come into the aerodrome.'

'Thank you, Ruth. It will help me get a bit more money together before I move on,' Emily had said.

***

Jenna

On Saturday morning, Emily decided to take a trip down to Charleville to do some shopping. Jenna waved them off; she was having a late start today as Ellie was going to open up for her. Josh wasn't coming for breakfast as he had the last three mornings, and was going to spend the morning with Amelia. She had got so used to his company; she was really going to miss him when he left next week.

She frowned. Josh lived so far away, there was no chance of a relationship. It wasn't as though they could catch up on weekends. It was going to hurt because Jenna knew she'd fallen hard and fast.

She made herself a cup of tea and took it back to bed and felt decadent as she snoozed until about 8:30. A knock on the door surprised her; who could be knocking at the door at this time of the morning?

Her heart leapt. Maybe it was Josh.

And Emily was gone for the morning. She pulled her robe over her summer pyjamas for decency's sake, fluffed up her hair, and peered out the living room window and hurried to the door, excited anticipation fizzing through her veins.

It wasn't Josh.

Mum and Dad's car was parked out front.

She opened the door with a smile. 'You're early, Mum.'

Her mother stood on the small front landing by herself. Jenna glanced over to the car. There was no sign of her father. Jenna frowned as Mum put her hand up to Jenna's cheek and stared at her.

'What's wrong, Mum? There's something wrong, isn't there?'

Her mother nodded mutely.

Jenna stepped back and held the door open as her mother walked inside. She stiffened, as her mother's arms went around her.

'Mum, what is it? Tell me. Is Dad okay?'

Her mother's voice was muffled, and she finally stepped back and looked at Jenna, tears rolling down her face. 'Dad's fine. He stayed at the aged care facility.'

Jenna kept staring at her, wondering what was wrong, and then she knew. 'It's Reg. Is he sick? I'll just get changed. Just wait for me, Mum.'

'There's no rush, sweetie. Your grandfather passed away through the night in his sleep.'

Tears sprang to Jenna's eyes. 'Oh, Mum. No. Not Reg. I can't believe it.'

Curling her fingers, she pushed the heels of her hands against her eyes to stop the tears. Stars filled her vision as she pressed hard, and Mum reached for her as she swayed. She buried her face into Mum's shoulder and they cried together.

Finally, Mum moved back a little and ran her hand over Jenna's hair. 'I know you won't want to work this morning. Do you think you should get Ellie to stay for the day and get one of the other girls in for the afternoon to help?'

'I will. I couldn't go to work now. I just

couldn't. I'll spend the day with you.'

'Do you want to come to the home to see him? He's still there.'

'Yes, Mum, I do,' Jenna said, shock making her shiver as she let go of her mother. 'I'll just take a quick shower.'

'I'll put the kettle on. I need a hot drink,' Mum said.

Jenna was quick in the shower, and a few minutes later, she was dressed. Mum had a teabag in a cup waiting for her, and they sat at the table together, both talking and occasionally crying.

'I still can't believe it, Mum, but I guess I should have been more prepared. He was old, wasn't he?'

'It'll be a shock to a lot of people, sweetie. He was just such an institution in this town. But we've got to look at the happy times we found with him. If you hadn't moved here, we would never have known about him, and we would never have had those couple of months with him.'

'I guess you're right, Mum. But even though we didn't know him long, I loved him.'

The day was spent at the home, seeing Dr. Harry and making arrangements with the funeral chapel down at Charleville to come up.

Together, she and Mum cleaned out his small cupboard. As Reg had told her a few weeks ago, he had very little.

Like he'd said, there was a shoebox on the shelf.

'He told me this was here only a short while ago. He said there was a box in there that he wanted me to have.'

'I know, he told me too that he wanted you to have it.'

Tears rolled down Mum's face as she folded Reg's other pair of pyjamas. 'We'll look later.'

'Do you think he knew his time was close, Mum?'

'I think he did. He got your dad to take him down to the solicitor in Charleville last week.'

'He told me he didn't have a will, because he had nothing, but now that he had you and me, he had everything.'

'That's why he went down with Dad.'

By the time Jenna got home at three-thirty she was totally drained. She'd call Josh later and meet him somewhere. As much as she wanted to have an early night and think about her time with her grandfather, she wanted to see Josh. She needed Josh.

As she stood at the kitchen window looking out over the dry lawn, the shock started to wear off and sadness set in.

Augathella without Reg wouldn't be the same, and for the first time, Jenna wondered if she did want to stay here. Mum and Dad would start travelling again, and everyone else here had their own families to be with.

Tears seeped from the corner of her eyes and she brushed them away angrily, before she smiled for a moment, imagining Reg saying, 'Chin up, lassie.'

She boiled the kettle; it wouldn't be long before Emily was home, and she always appreciated a cup of tea.

A car pulled up outside, and she flicked the kettle back on to bring it to the boil, then walked to the door. She didn't want to frighten Emily, who wouldn't be expecting her to be home yet, although she would have seen her car in the carport. She opened the door for her, and stopped in surprise as Luke bounded up the front steps. She stared mutely and her eyes filled with tears.

'What are you doing here?' She shook her head as tears rolled down her face,

'Jenna, are you okay?' Luke stepped forward

and put his arms around her. 'It's okay. When you can get your breath, tell me what's wrong.'

She leaned into his shoulder, sobbing.

The sound of another car turning into the driveway made her lift her head, and she stepped back as Emily drove into the other side of the carport.

'Come inside, Luke. I'll make a cup of tea.' She forced a smile through her tears. 'It's all I seem to do lately. Make cups of tea for comfort. I had some bad news this morning. I haven't been to work. My grandad passed away through the night, and my parents and I have been dealing with it all day.'

'I'm so sorry to hear that. Sit down, and I'll make the tea.'

'Make a pot, please. It's on the sink, just waiting to be warmed. The tea leaves are in the caddy on the shelf above the kettle. You have to meet Emily. She and her little girl are sharing the apartment with me now that Alana's moved out.'

***

Emily hesitated as she went around to the back door to lift Ophelia out of the car. She smiled as two arms reached up to her. 'Mama. Jenna play?' Ophelia asked with a big smile.

Ophelia had fallen in love with Jenna. They spent a lot of time playing on the living room floor before Jenna left with Josh for dinner each night. Emily appreciated the help as she cooked Ophelia's dinner. She wasn't sure why Jenna was home, and she wondered who'd been hugging her on the porch as she'd driven in. The man was too tall for Josh.

Emily bit her lip. Surely, Jenna would have known that she was coming home now, so she wasn't going to walk in on anything.

Hopefully.

With a shrug, she lifted Ophelia out and reached for her bag that was next to the baby seat.

They walked slowly across to the front steps, Ophelia pointing at the different flowers and saying, 'Blue, yellow, pink.'

'You're such a clever girl,' Emily said. They had both settled into Augathella so well. Emily was even considering perhaps accepting work after Christmas if there was work available at the school.

They walked slowly up the front stairs, and the front door was still open, but Emily stood there and tapped on the door before they went inside. 'Jenna, it's me. You're home early.'

'We're in the kitchen, Em. Come on in.' Her voice sounded strained. Emily put her bag on the sofa in the living room as she carried Ophelia into the kitchen.

Her eyes widened when she saw Jenna's red-rimmed eyes and puffy eyelids.

'Jenna, is everything okay?' She went to take a step forward and realised the man she'd seen was standing at the fridge.

She turned her head and stifled a horrified gasp. The blood left her head and her head spun so much, she bent and put Ophelia on the floor. Unusually, she started to grizzle, sensing the tension in the room.

Luke? How could Luke Elliott be here in Jenna's kitchen? How had he found where she was?

Emily blinked and forced herself to look again. She wasn't wrong. She had to swallow to stop herself gagging. As she turned to the window trying desperately to compose herself, her fingers closed around the car keys, in case she had to make a quick escape.

'It's okay, Emily. My grandad died this morning. I haven't been to work.' Jenna put her hands over her eyes and wasn't looking at either Emily or Luke as their eyes met.

Luke blanched and his mouth dropped open.

'Oh, and this is a friend of mine, Luke.'

Emily turned away slowly, Ophelia hanging onto her leg. She didn't know what to do. She didn't know what to say. She didn't know whether to let on to Jenna that she knew Luke Elliott. Luke must have seen the uncertainty on her face before she turned away, and he held out his hand.

'Hello, Emily, is it? It's nice to meet you.'

Emily just nodded as Luke stared at Ophelia, and then back at her. His expression held grief.

CHAPTER 18

Emily

'I'll just go and bath Ophelia,' Emily said.

'I'll be going out shortly,' Jenna said. 'I'm sorry Luke, I'm busy tonight. I should be home later, but would you be right if I wasn't, Emily?'

'We'll be fine, but you take care.' Emily left Luke and Jenna in the living room.

If she had the house to herself, that would be much better. Being Friday night, she had the weekend ahead, and maybe she had some big decisions to make. What was Luke doing here? It appeared that he knew Jenna well. Was it just a coincidence that he'd turned up in the town she was in? Jenna had never mentioned Luke.

She trawled through her thoughts, through all those memories, both happy and sad, and then pushed them away, realising how stupid she was being. Luke was a good man but he knew too much of her past.

Emily didn't want anybody to know where she was. She didn't want anyone to know what had happened. It was hard enough here with all these damn pilots around. Fallon was a helicopter pilot, and Josh, Amelia's brother, flew both helicopters and planes. It was the last thing she needed to think about.

Those days were in the past, and she needed to move on. She needed to get over it. She needed to find somewhere where she and Ophelia could start a new life, a place where she could get a job, suitable daycare, and earn enough money to make a good life for them. Tears welled up in her eyes, and she brushed them away angrily. Ophelia started splashing in the bathwater, and Emily blinked. She'd been so wrapped up in her thoughts that she couldn't remember undressing her little girl and putting her in the water. How dreadful. What if she'd slipped, and she hadn't been paying attention? But when she looked down, she realised that her hand was on Ophelia's little bare back, and she was splashing in the water and grinning up at her mummy.

'I do love you so much, little one,' she said. 'We're going to be alright, aren't we? We are.'

She'd often wondered if Luke would come looking for her. It weighed on her, an explanation. He and Troy had been really good mates when they'd all been at high school, and she was sure that he would know about the accident. But she was also sure that he wouldn't know all of the horrible details that came afterwards.

The details that meant Troy's life insurance hadn't come through, and the small estate he'd left behind was still caught up in the throes of the legal machine. When it did come through, it probably wouldn't be enough for them to start anew. Neither of them had had any family, and that was what had brought her and Troy together in the first place. If only she had known what his state of mind was, and what he was hiding. If only she had known that she would be a widow at twenty-seven.

She looked down at her precious little girl looking up at her, and realised that even if she had known, she wouldn't have given away the chance to have her beautiful child.

'Emily Jansen, you just have to toughen up and get on with life,' she murmured.

If Luke Elliott came to see her, she would deal with it then.

CHAPTER 18

Jenna

When Luke left, Emily was still in the bathroom with Ophelia, and Jenna knew he could tell by looking at her what she was thinking.

'I think you know, Luke, it's nice to have you as a friend, but that's all we can ever be. I've met somebody else, and I realise now what I should have been feeling with you. But please, let's stay friends.'

Luke's eyes were hooded as he nodded. He spoke quietly, 'Of course. But can you tell me about Emily. Where is she from?'

Jenna shrugged. 'I don't know much; she's only been in town for ten days or so. She's starting work at the primary school after the holidays. Why do you ask?'

Luke shook his head, 'I was just curious. Does she have a new partner?'

'A new partner?' Jenna frowned.

Luke shook his head. 'Sorry I meant a partner.''

'I don't know. As far as I know, it's just her and Ophelia.'

Luke leaned over and brushed his lips over her cheek. 'I wish you all the best. Take care of yourself, Jenna, won't you?'

'I will, Luke.'

As soon as Luke had gone, Emily came out of the bathroom. Jenna had a shower and washed her hair, letting the steaming hot water run over her face, soothing some of the soreness around her eyes and easing her sadness a little bit. She didn't know whether to ring Joshua or just go around to Amelia and Ben's house. The word was probably getting around town now about Reg, and it was going to be hard to talk to anybody she ran into, her grief was so raw. All Jenna knew was that she wanted Josh to be holding her.

The depth of her feelings amazed her; how could she have such strong feelings for him after knowing him for little more than a week? It was like one of those movies that used to make her shake her head in disbelief. She had read about people meeting and falling for each other straight away, and she knew what she was feeling was real. She'd had several other semi-relationships over the years, and she'd never had this intensity of feeling before. The problem was they had to sort out what was going to happen because she knew that Josh felt the same way about her; he didn't have to tell her; she just knew.

Jenna scrubbed her face with the washer, rinsed her hair, and when she was out of the shower and dried, she rubbed moisturiser around her puffy eyes. She wound her wet hair up into a roll on the back of her head and walked to her room with a towel around her. She chose a pair of jeans and a long-sleeved T-shirt because it was still a little bit cool at night.

Emily was sitting in the kitchen, feeding Ophelia her vegetables when Jenna came out of her room. Emily stood and put Ophelia on her hip, and with her other arm, she reached out and hugged Jenna.

'I'm so sorry to hear about your granddad, Jenna.'

'Thank you. I'm still getting used to the news, but I'm okay. Emily, can I be honest with you?'

Emily was surprised and her eyes widened; she looked around the room as if looking for someone.

'Luke's gone?' she asked.

Jenna replied, 'Yes. He's gone.'

'Where do you know him from, Jenna?'

Jenna found it interesting that both Luke and Emma were so interested in each other, having just met. 'Oh, he's a pilot friend; he flies in here for work. Braden and Kent brought him along to the opening of the tearooms. He works out with Braden, Kent, and Jon on their properties. We have a bit of a friendship, that's all it was.'

'Ah, I see.'

'Why do you ask?' Even though Jenna had been emotional, she had picked up the tension between Luke and Emily.

'Oh, no reason, just interested. Anyway, what were you going to say to me? You said you wanted to be honest with me.'

'I won't be home tonight, Emily.'

'You said that before. You do whatever you have to do. I'm sure your mum and dad will need your company.'

Jenna shrugged. 'It's not Mum and Dad. I'm going to spend the night with Josh. I need . . . I need time with him.'

Emily's smile was sad. She patted Jenna's shoulder. 'If you know what you need, Jen, you go for it. We should all do that. One day, when you're feeling less sad, I'll tell you my story.'

'I'll look forward to it.'

Emily reached out and hugged her.

'Thanks Emily. Have a good night, won't you?'

Emily smiled. 'And you have the best night ever, Jenna.'

CHAPTER 19

Emily

Emily knew that Luke would come; she was sure of it. As sure as the sun would rise in the morning and set in the afternoon. She knew that Luke would want to help her; he wouldn't let her go, even though she had made the dreadful mistake of letting him go.

Ophelia was asleep, and Emily was sitting in the living room with the lights out when there was a soft knock on the door. She'd showered, put on one of her best dresses, and waited for him to arrive.

She opened the door, and Luke walked in without speaking. Slowly, his hands reached out to her, and she stepped into his embrace. Having her face on his shoulder, with his arms holding her tightly, filled her with a peace that she hadn't felt for more than three years.

'I've been looking for you for a long time, Emily. It was hard to find you. They said you moved away as soon as Troy died.'

'I did,' she said softly.

'I couldn't find you. Where did you go?'

'I went to a little town called Ravenshoe on the Atherton Tablelands. There's a small cottage hospital there. I had enough money to rent a little house, and when I gave birth to Ophelia, we stayed there for six months.'

'What are you doing in Augathella?'

'I'm on the way to my new life. Maybe South Australia. I don't know where. I wanted to get as far away from Townsville as I could and away from Narrabri too.'

'That makes me sad to hear. Why would you want to get away from Narrabri?'

'Too many memories, Luke. Too many memories of bad choices. That's where I made the mistake of marrying Troy.'

He stared at her, his eyes sad.

'Don't look at me like that. I know it was a mistake. I should've chosen you. You should know. If only I'd known what he was really like.'

'Did he ever hurt you, Emily?'

'Not physically, but he had a very sharp tongue. When he found out I was pregnant, things changed for the worse.'

'Tell me about the crash.'

She lifted her eyes, stepped back, and stared at him. She knew straight away that he suspected what really happened.

'I can't.'

'It was suicide, wasn't it?'

She nodded slowly. 'It was, Luke. I've come to terms with it now, and I can't take any responsibility for it. Troy had mental health issues. The thought that he killed others with his selfishness is something I can't forget.'

'He had a good reason to be disturbed, Emily. I don't know if you knew about his childhood background before you moved to Narrabri when we were in high school.'

'No, his parents were both dead by the time I moved to town. When we were married, I used to hear him calling out for his mother in the night.'

'I'll tell you about it one day,' he said.

She nodded. 'Maybe.'

'Do you think I'm going to let you go now that I've finally found you? I can't believe that you're here. I walked in, and I thought I was seeing the vision that I've been wanting to see for over two years now.'

'I thought you were with Jenna for a moment and pain ripped through me.'

'I only came here because Jenna and I have struck up a friendship.'

'She told me you were only friends. I

wondered though, when I saw you hugging her on the veranda.'

'She'd just told me about her grandfather's death. She's a good person. And then when I walked into the kitchen, I saw you.'

'I didn't know what to do,' she said.

He smiled. 'I know you so well, Emily.'

'I know, Luke.' She sighed. 'But I'm not good enough for you. I will never forgive myself for leaving you.'

'I know, Emily. But I also know how charismatic Troy could be when he wanted something. And when he saw that we were falling in love, he wanted you.'

Tears filled Emily's eyes as she looked up at Luke.

'I never gave up looking. I knew that it wouldn't last with Troy. I knew he would tire of you, but I never dreamed that his demons would catch up with him like they did.' Luke smoothed her hair back from her face. 'We need to talk, and we need to talk about the future. Can I ask you to do that with me? When the time is right? When you feel comfortable?'

The peace that had fallen over Emily when she was sitting there, waiting for Luke to come, grew, and the lightness of her being was a totally new feeling for her.

'We can talk about it, but not now. I've got commitments here for the next ten weeks. I won't be going anywhere in that time.'

'I can live with that,' he said. 'I have to visit here a lot over the next few months. I've just taken over the supervision of the cattle sales on another three properties. In fact, I could probably get a room at the pub and stay here for a month or so now.'

Emily smiled and reached her hand up to his face. 'That will give us a lot of time to talk.'

'It will, Emily.' His arms wrapped around

her, and her head rested on his shoulder. Something had led her to this little town for a reason and she knew she had come home in more ways than one.

CHAPTER 20

Jenna

When Jenna opened the little wooden box that night, her world shifted. She stared down at the small pink diamond, and then she cried again as she read Reg's spidery writing.

His note was short. 'I found this diamond on the ground many years ago in the north. Take it and live the life you want to, my darling girl.'

She sat for a long time before she left home and walked to Amelia and Ben's house.

The lights were on as Jenna walked up the front path, Chilli Girl beside her. Before she could knock on the door, it opened and Josh stepped out, closing the door quietly behind him. His arms wrapped around her and he held her tightly. 'I'm so sorry, Jen. I just heard the news from Ben.'

'It's been an awful day. My tears have gone,' she said. 'I don't think I can cry anymore.'

They stood there quietly, their heads together, Josh holding her close. 'I've been thinking about us today, about lots of things, even before I heard the news. I don't want to leave, Jenna. I don't think I can leave you.'

Her eyes met his, and her smile was tremulous. 'You're certainly not going to go and leave me, Joshua Foley.'

'I'm not.'

'Because wherever you're going, I'm going with you.'

'Where to?'

'To Darwin, Granite Springs, wherever you're going, I'm going with you.'

'What about your tearoom?'

'That's not important to me. Finding my grandfather so late in life and then losing him so quickly has taught me a very good lesson. When you love somebody, you spend time with them, you don't put other things first, not your career, a business, or anything. I want to come with you.'

Josh's face lit up with the biggest smile Jenna had seen yet. 'You know people are going to think we're crazy, being with each other for only ten days.'

'I don't care what people think, Josh. *I* think I'm crazy. I know Mum and Dad are going to think I'm crazy. But you know what? I don't care. I want to come with you.'

'I want you to come with me too, but I never would have asked you,' he said.

'You know, there's something else I want to ask you.' Jenna looped her arms around Josh's neck.

'Something else? Nothing could be better than telling me you're coming with me.'

'Maybe not quite so early in the night, but later on when the bistro is empty, how would you like to go to the hotel?'

His face brightened. 'You mean stay the night at the pub?'

She nodded. 'Yes, please.'

'I think that's the best idea I've heard for a long time,' he said.

Josh pulled her close and her lips met his. Jenna's grief eased as happiness consumed her.

CHAPTER 21

Two weeks later

The last day of spring in the small town of Augathella marked the culmination of a big week for the town. On Monday, local identity, Reg, known affectionately as the Augathella Fella had been farewelled in a moving service at the local church and then interred in the local cemetery.

On the same day, Emily Jansen started her new career at the primary school after happily leaving Ophelia at Ruth's house.

During the preceding two weeks, the town gossips had been interested in the time that Luke, the manager from Dwyer Holdings, had spent in Emily's company.

On Wednesday, there was a ceremony at the hotel when a brass plaque was fixed to the wall above the chair that Reg had claimed for many years. Jenna and her parents had been chuffed when the mayor had come up from Charleville for the ceremony.

On Thursday, Jenna's parents stood at the aerodrome and farewelled their daughter as she left town in Joshua Foley's plane. Josh promised they would be back within the month because he was going home to tell his dad that he'd bought a property adjacent to Braden Cartwright's station. Jenna had argued, saying he didn't have to leave Granite Springs just for her, but Josh insisted.

'It's what I want, Jenna,' he'd said, 'and I want to see you still running Jenna's Vintage Tea Rooms. For a while at least.'

Ellie was looking after the tearooms in Jenna's absence.

Saturday, the day of the Spring Fair dawned bright and clear.

Gladys Tingle shook her head as they stood in Jenny Riley's garden on Saturday morning. 'I don't know what's happening in this town, but I see young girls coming here and taking up with young chaps straight away.'

Beryl replied, 'You're just jealous, Gladys.'

Gladys retorted, 'I've never told you that I had a bit of a fling a lot of years ago with Reg. Now that he's passed, I can tell. You didn't know that, did you?'

'Get out of here. You're making that up,' Beryl said.

'That'll give you something to think about.' Glady's smile was smug.

On this beautiful spring Saturday, Jenny Riley's RFDS Spring Fair was a huge success. Children ran happily up and down between the avenues of roses as they moved from the clowns to the pony rides and the face painting. The crowds came from faraway places like Tambo, Charleville, and even Cunnamulla. They partook of delicious cakes that Jenna had spent two weeks making before she'd flown north with Josh. The highlight of the day was when Doctor Harry and his fiancée, Laura were seen heading for the hospital when Amelia Riley and Sophie Mason went into labour within minutes of each other.

***

Callie and Braden parked outside Ruth's house when they left the fair. Ruth had offered to mind the boys while they went to the hospital to visit Sophie. Jon and Fallon were there too, and Fallon insisted that Callie leave the twins as well.

'The more the merrier,' she said. 'Give Sophie and Kent our love,' she called after them as they hurried back to the car.

As they parked at the hospital, Jenny and Tom Riley followed them into the car park.

Callie waited until they were out of the car. 'News?' she asked.

'A baby boy, twenty minutes ago. Ben just

called and told us to come straight up. Sophie?' Jenny asked.

'A baby girl, twenty minutes ago. Kent just called.'

'Oh, my goodness, Harry and Laura have been busy. I'm so pleased they decided to stay in town.'

Callie and Braden walked quietly down the corridor, and Laura met them at the nurse's station.

'Just a very quick visit to say hello to your new niece. She still has to be weighed and checked over.'

'Is everything okay?' Braden asked. 'Is Sophie alright?'

'Yes, Mum and bub . . . and Dad are doing well.'

Callie's eyes pricked with tears as she watched Braden hurry across the room and kiss his sister's cheek. She could hear the tears thick in his throat as he spoke. 'Well done, sis, I love you.'

'I'm a real mum now,' Sophie said.

'You've always been a real mum,' Braden said as he hugged her.

THE END

Come back to Augathella for Christmas . . .

Pre-orders available for:

An Augathella Christmas

eBook:

https://www.amazon.com.au/gp/product/B0CL L1DNZB

200

OTHER PRINT BOOKS from ANNIE

Available on Annie's store and Amazon:

https://annieseatonstore.ecwid.com/

New Series: The Daughters of The Darling

1: From Across the Sea (April 2024)

2. Over the River (September 2024)

Other books

Whitsunday Dawn

Undara

Osprey Reef

East of Alice

Porter Sisters Series

Kakadu Sunset

Daintree

Diamond Sky

Hidden Valley

Larapinta

Kakadu Dawn

Pentecost Island Series

Pippa

Eliza

Nell

Tamsin

Evie

Cherry

Odessa

Sienna

Tess

Isla

Also available in three boxed sets

Books 1-3

Books 4-6

Books 7-10

The Augathella Girls Series

Outback Roads

Outback Sky

Outback Escape

Outback Wind

Outback Dawn

Outback Moonlight

Outback Dust

Outback Hope

Sunshine Coast Series

Waiting for Ana

The Trouble with Jack

Healing His Heart

Sunshine Coast Boxed Set

The Richards Brothers Series

The Trouble with Paradise

Marry in Haste

Outback Sunrise

Richards Brothers Boxed Set

Bondi Beach Love Series

Beach House

Beach Music

Beach Walk

Beach Dreams

The House on the Hill

Second Chance Bay Series

Her Outback Playboy

Her Outback Protector

Her Outback Haven

Her Outback Paradise

The McDougalls of Second Chance Bay

Boxed Set

Love Across Time Series

Come Back to Me

Follow Me

Finding Home

The Threads that Bind

Love Across Time 1-4 Boxed Set

Bindarra Creek

Worth the Wait

Full Circle

Secrets of River Cottage

A Clever Christmas

A Bindarra Creek Duo

A Place to Belong

Four Seasons Short and Sweet

Ten Days in Paradise

Follow the Sun

Others

Deadly Secrets

Adventures in Time

Silver Valley Witch

The Emerald Necklace

Christmas with the Boss

Her Christmas Star

An Aussie Christmas Duo (the two Christmas novellas)

ABOUT THE AUTHOR

Annie lives in Australia, on the beautiful north coast of New South Wales. She sits in her writing chair and looks out over the tranquil Pacific Ocean.

She writes contemporary romance and loves telling stories that always have a happily ever after. She lives with her very own hero of many years and they share their home with Toby, the naughtiest dog in the universe, and Barney, the ragdoll puss, who hides when the four grandchildren come to visit.

Stay up to date with her latest releases at her website: http://www.annieseaton.net

AWARDS

2023: Winner of the long contemporary RUBY award for Larapinta

Finalist for the NZ KORU award 2018 and 2020.

Winner ...Best Established Author of the Year 2017 AUSROM

Long listed for the Sisters in Crime Davitt Awards 2016, 2017, 2018, 2019

Finalist in Book of the Year, Long Romance, RWA Ruby Awards 2016 Kakadu Sunset

Winner ...Best Established Author of the Year 2015 AUSROM

Winner ...Author of the Year 2014 AUSROM

Best Established Author, Ausrom Readers' Choice 2017 Book of the Year